SAVANNAH J. FRIERSON

AJ's Serendipity

SJF BOOKS

To finding love when and where you least expect it.

Acknowledgments

It's been a decade since I introduced readers to AJ and Samara's story, and a lot has changed. Specifically, I have grown as a writer; and as I revisited this story, I realized I made some new-writer mistakes. Now that I am older, wiser, and over ten years into this business, I hope this fresh edit and update for *AJ's Serendipity* will meet an even larger audience while reflecting where we have moved both as an author and as a reading public. I really like this story, y'all, and I really am grateful Aliyah Burke (http://www.aliyah-burke.com) let me borrow her beloved Megalodon Team characters to tell this tale.

I'd also like to thank Dominique Lambright for the editing and Raquel Erbach for the cover art! I'm so thrilled to have worked with you ladies.

Finally, I would like to give a big thank you to my Patreon supporters, my newsletter subscribers, and my family and friends. Special shout-out to my sister, *Dr.* Karma Frierson. This one's for you!

ONE

AJ Melonakos didn't register the splat of newly purchased tomatoes upon the stone walkway, his attention completely on the woman he'd spotted two booths down. She was clearly an American, for Americans tended to stick out like sore thumbs, especially in Greece. It was the way she carried herself—cautious, but not nearly cautious enough, as if someone wouldn't have the unmitigated gall to approach her and do something untoward. She was looking at the wares being sold at Monastiraki. It was clear she wasn't really interested in buying anything, but she gave the vendors shy smiles and nodded when appropriate. And before AJ realized what he was doing, he shook off the tomato carcasses from his foot and began to follow her, ignoring the vendor screeching God knew what as he left.

She was a black woman, her skin not as deeply rich as he had seen with other women, but there was a medium-brown hue to her smooth skin that shone beautifully against the pink sundress she wore. The straps were thin, and her chest seemed bountiful in the bodice.

Her hair was in that natural Afro style, and a cliff rose flower was tucked behind her ear. She was not the most beautiful woman he had ever seen, nor would she grace a high-fashion magazine cover in the near future, but she was his very definition of a woman: soft, lush, delicately strong.

She was oblivious to the looks other men were giving her, as if unaware she could enchant someone the way she was. If she wanted someone to help her discover all the treasures she possessed, AJ was more than willing to offer his services. He was nothing if not an ardent and enthusiastic explorer of the female form.

She stopped at another booth where flowers were sold. She took time to smell them, clearly pleased by the scent of the orchids she picked up. The vendor spoke to her, telling her more about the flora.

"Thank you," he saw her mouth form, and the corners of his own turned up.

She had bewitched AJ completely, and that bewildered him. Something about her called to him, that shyness and vulnerability he saw. Unable to ignore it, he found himself approaching the booth, his lips quirking slightly when she remained ever cautious, yet oblivious to his focus on her.

"I'd like a bouquet for the lady," he said in English to the vendor, wanting this enchantress to know he meant the gift for her. She looked at him with another cursory smile, though her eyes widened. Brown eyes. They were oval-shaped and a sweet, pretty brown, deep and rich. She looked behind her, then glanced his way once more before telling the vendor thank you again and leaving.

He was confused as the vendor gave him the flowers, until he looked to his right and saw an attractive brunette woman also perusing the booth. AJ chuckled to himself. His charming pink lady had assumed he wasn't referring to her. Well, he would find her and let her know otherwise.

She wasn't hard to track. There weren't many people of color in the market, and the pink outfit was like a beacon to him. She stopped in front of another booth full of paintings, but her posture was one of, "I'm just browsing, won't be staying long."

Before AJ allowed her to get away from him again, he approached, calling out to her since her back was to him.

"Miss, you forgot your flowers."

She didn't respond, didn't even turn to look at him. She continued looking at the knockoff portraits at her feet, her brows furrowed and her fingers tapping at her lips. He chuckled to himself, unable to believe this woman was so lost in her own world. That could be dangerous, especially since she was foreign and traveling alone. She would need an escort.

He volunteered himself.

AJ went closer to her, this time bending his six-foot-two frame so he could speak in her ear. She hadn't seemed so short at a distance. "You forgot something."

She gasped and jumped, her breath coming out harshly. She placed a hand on her chest as if it could slow down her heart rate. "You scared me!"

"I apologize," he said, his smile positively roguish as he held out the bouquet he had bought her. "You forgot these."

"I didn't buy any flowers," she said suspiciously, glancing at his eyes and the flowers before beginning to turn away.

"I know. I did. For you."

That had her turning back to him, but her expression was wary, downright mistrustful. "For me?"

"Yes."

She frowned at him. "Why?"

"You liked them. I wanted you to have them."

Her frown deepened, and she looked at the vendor as if he could clarify things for her. The vendor merely shrugged and went to help another customer. "You wasted your money."

"No such thing. Come. Take the flowers. I insist."

"But I thought that woman—"

"You were the only woman I saw."

Her eyes fluttered, and she took in a deep breath. "Are you flirting with me?"

"Trying to," he said with a devilish smile. She bit her lip to hide her grin and rolled her eyes, but he cheered internally, knowing this short, spitfire of a woman thought him humorous.

"Are you trying to sell me something? Did you target me as gullible? This happened to me in Egypt once...got a marriage proposal too."

"Pity you turned him down," he said with mock sadness, "but he obviously has impeccable taste to want to spend the rest of his life with you."

She scowled. "That was pretty thick."

He quirked an eyebrow. "You have no idea, sweetheart."

She bit her lip again and was even less successful hiding her grin. She crossed her arms underneath her chest, only serving to enhance her gorgeous cleavage, but he made himself look into her eyes.

Her deep-brown eyes.

"You know you want to take the flowers," he said, coming closer to her. She leaned back, but didn't move otherwise, and he was heartened even more. "And if you'd like to be even less of a target, I could escort you."

"Escort me where?"

He shrugged. "Anywhere you'd like to go. A beautiful woman such as yourself shouldn't be alone, anyway. Your husband must be a fool."

"Are you serious?"

"About him being a fool?"

"About—" She abruptly cut off her speech and shook her head. "Never mind. I really must be going, but thank you for the offer—"

"AJ," he interrupted. "My name is AJ."

"AJ," she said, as if testing it out on her tongue. Her suspicious demeanor gave a little and she shrugged, holding out her hand. "I'm Samara."

AJ took her hand and brought it to his lips. "A wonderful pleasure to meet you, Miss Samara."

"Miss? Just a few seconds ago you had me married."

"Are you?"

She gave a wry chuckle. "I'm not sure how that's relevant."

"It's relevant because I'd like to invite you to dinner with me and I want to make sure it's a table for two instead of three."

She giggled, and it was the cutest sound he'd ever heard. "Okay. Can I have my hand back?"

He let go of her hand immediately, if reluctantly. "Please accept these flowers. It's a gift without any strings."

"Why don't I believe that?"

"Because you are an American, and Americans are as gullible as they are suspicious."

That bottom lip went between her teeth again, and AJ wondered how it would feel between his. He wanted to pull her close, fit her to him, protect her. There would be no reason to be suspicious as long as he was around.

She shrugged again and held out the hand he'd just let go. "Okay. I accept. Thank you."

He smiled and placed the stems in her hands, making sure his fingertips glanced her palm. Her eyelids fluttered again as she stared at him and his heart swelled. He knew he was a handsome man. He'd often been told that his golden-tan skin, green eyes, and thick black hair made him appealing; but something about her awed expression humbled him and made him feel pride at the same time. He was glad she found him pleasing.

His broadening smile seemed to break her out of whatever trance she'd been in and she hid her face in the bouquet. "This was very sweet of you."

"You're the sweet one."

She snorted, shaking her head. "You don't know me well enough to make a judgment call like that."

"Would you let me?"

"Let you what?"

"Get to know you a little better?"

She took a deep breath, staring at the flowers for a long moment, then lifted her eyes to scan the marketplace. "Okay."

"Really?" The excitement and surprise in the word made him wince, but he'd been preparing for her refusal. He would've invited her to his restaurant anyway, free and clear, if only just to see her one last time.

"As long as we stay here in Monastiraki, then yes. I have about an hour left before I have to leave."

"Then let's go," he said, offering her his hand this time. She peered at it, but simply smiled and started walking. AJ chuckled. He'd have to earn her touch? So be it.

As they walked and shopped, he told her of the history of the market. She asked questions that told him she had a very inquisitive mind and loved history. She also began to relax, meeting his eyes more as they spoke. Of course, she'd get a blush on her cheeks and avert her attention quickly, but he wouldn't rush her.

"'Allo! Lovely young couple, there! Paint you and the wife!"

Once again, Samara kept walking, or would have, had AJ not stopped and touched her elbow to gain her attention.

"Yes?" she asked.

"This artist would like to paint us."

She looked at him, confused, then at the painter who lifted up his brush and palette and nodded enthusiastically. "Paint us?"

"Yes! Paint a beautiful couple!"

"Oh, we're not—"

"Come on, darling," AJ said, his green eyes darkening in challenge. "He is very talented, no? Though da Vinci himself wouldn't be able to capture your beauty."

She rolled her eyes and shook her head. "So bad."

"I assure you, precious," AJ began, bending his mouth to her ear, the hairs of his trim goatee tickling her skin, "bad is not a critique I've ever gotten."

"You're getting it now," she said, smirking slightly.

He grinned, showing his even, white teeth, and tilted his head toward the artist. "Please. Let's do the painting. I'll even pay."

"And you'll keep it?"

"Unless you want it."

Her eyes dropped to his chest, and she let out a long-suffering sigh. "You really want the painting."

"I do."

Samara closed her eyes and almost let her forehead drop to his chest before she caught herself. "Okay."

AJ sent up silent thanks for allowing this painter to extend his time with her. Because there was only one stool, AJ sat down first and, after much coaxing and the serendipitous discovery she was insanely ticklish, settled Samara into his lap. She was rigid at first, understandable since he was still a stranger.

"Relax, precious," he whispered into her ear.

"Relax?"

"I won't bite unless you give me permission."

That broke her tension and she laughed, settling into him. She cradled the flowers in her arms like a newborn. Unable to help himself, he rested his chin against her temple and held her gently. He would have rocked her if they didn't need to remain still. Some people began to stop and stare at them, and Samara grew uncomfortable. She started wiggling, and he pressed a hand to her hip with a hiss.

"You cannot do that, sweetheart."

She turned her head to look at him. "Do what?"

"Wiggle that delicious bum in my lap. You'll make me forget I'm trying to be a gentleman."

"Oh! I'm sorry!"

He smiled and trailed a finger down her cheek. "I don't want you uncomfortable. Just want you to have a good time."

Gazing into each other's eyes, AJ slowly linked his fingers through hers and was glad she didn't pull her hand away. They remained that way for the rest of the sitting, both ignoring the crowd, the painter, and the fact their hour was dangerously close to expiring. His thumb caressed her hand, and he wanted to kiss her so badly. He thought she wanted it, too, considering the way she licked her lips intermittingly. But he didn't want their first kiss to be in front of an audience; so, when the painter finally said he was finished, he winked at her and helped her to her feet.

"How much?" AJ asked in Greek.

"I give it to you free," the painter said, glancing at Samara briefly. "It's always nice to see a young couple in love."

AJ's heart constricted at that, but he smiled and thanked the man. He took the painting after the artist rolled it up carefully and gave the man a tip anyway. He turned around to see Samara still waiting, eyeing the painting in his hand.

"Will I get a chance to see it?"

He gave her a coy smile. "Maybe."

"Maybe!"

He chuckled and held out his hand. After a brief hesitation, she took it. He squeezed her hand in gratitude.

Now, the two merely strolled, she taking in the sights and he taking in her. Love...he couldn't possibly be in love with her, not just yet. Nevertheless, AJ suspected Samara was the kind of woman who made it easy to fall in love her and not have a man regret it. He sensed a goodness about her, an honesty he couldn't help but be charmed by.

He led them into a side street where there was less pedestrian traffic. "How much of that hour do we have left?"

Samara looked at her watch and sucked her teeth. "I have to go now."

"Where are you staying?"

"Why do you want to know?"

"To escort you there, of course."

She gave him a small grin. "I walked here alone."

"Shame, that is. You will indulge me in this, won't you, precious?"

Her grin widened and she inclined her head deferentially. "Marina Hotel."

It was not too far from the market, but it was still a nice enough walk that he could play tour guide and point to all the places of interest that might not be in a travel book. When they reached the destination, both weren't very thrilled.

"Will I see you again?"

She turned to him and he internally cheered when she didn't drop his hand. "Really?"

"Definitely, precious."

She shook her head. "I'm not here alone."

He winced, unable to help it. Could it be she actually *was* taken? He hoped not. The connection he felt with Samara...he couldn't promise not to be a cad and not to try to lure her away.

"Then you should come to my restaurant," he said with a slightly forced smile. "I promise to give you a good deal."

"Ah, so there *was* an angle!"

She was teasing him; but for a quick moment, a defense had sprung on his tongue. He gave her a slow grin and touched the tip of her nose affectionately. "You think you are so witty, precious."

"I've been known to have a way with words."

"I'll say," he murmured, his eyes staring at her mouth. He stared for so long that she bit that bottom lip once more, and he found himself grazing it with his thumb. She gasped, clearly shocked by his boldness. So was he. He dropped his hand and stepped back quickly.

"I took liberties. I'm sorry."

She said nothing, allowing the silence to stretch until he could only nod and turn on his heel like a chastised puppy.

"AJ?"

He paused. "Yes, Samara."

"What's the name of your restaurant?"

The tightness that had been growing in his chest loosened at her question, and he smiled, tucking the painting underneath his arm as he placed his hands in the pockets of his trousers and turned to face her again.

"Melonakos," AJ murmured. "It's my last name too."

She nodded and arched an eyebrow. "Is the food good?"

"The best you'll find on the peninsula."

She grinned and nodded again. "Hmm, guess I should see for myself."

"Great," he said, smiling as well. "I recommend coming at six, right before the evening rush. I'll reserve the best table for you."

"VIP, huh?"

"The most important person," AJ amended with a wink.

A laugh tumbled out and she shook her head. "All right, Mr. Melonakos. We'll see you at six."

"I eagerly anticipate the hour," AJ said. He didn't leave until long after she had disappeared into the hotel, bouncing the painting in his free hand. He didn't care he hadn't gotten what he'd originally gone to the market for. What he'd left with was so much better.

TWO

Though it was a warm enough evening, AJ opted to have Samara's table inside. It was tucked away in a private corner that provided intimacy and a lovely view of the street. Part of him wondered if he were defeating the purpose by allowing her and her...*guest*...such a setting, but he only wanted the best for Samara. Maybe there was a possibility she could realize *he* was the best as well.

The place was mostly empty since the dinner rush wouldn't get started until seven, but many regulars were here already to beat the crowd. He was courteous to all he greeted, but his eyes never strayed far from the restaurant's entrance. It was getting perilously close to six.

When Samara arrived two minutes after the top of the hour, his knees almost buckled with relief. The guest was a woman who looked so similar it was obvious they were related. Equally stunning, the other woman's hair was straight, but cut short in a sophisticated style. She had the curves her sister possessed, as evidenced by the strapless, A-line, black-and-white dress she wore, though she was slightly taller and not quite as round. Her demeanor screamed, "Don't look at me unless..." AJ didn't exactly know what the "unless" would be, but he bet it would take a strong, confident lover to discover it.

But it was the first woman who captured his attention and refused to let it go.

Samara had changed into wide-leg black slacks and a white peasant top showing off the thin, dark strap of a tank top. Due to the lighting and how far away they were, he couldn't tell the color. She had one of his orchids behind her ear, too, and he couldn't help but grin. All he wanted to do was hold her face in his hands and stare into her deep-brown eyes, but he was on the job, and he had no idea if the other woman knew about him.

She would soon find out.

His cousin Anatole started to lead them in the opposite direction, so he quickly hurried over to intercept.

"I've got it," he rumbled, his eyes still transfixed on the two American women, one in particular.

With a quirked eyebrow, Anatole left to attend to another group of customers that had just entered, but AJ barely noticed. He put his hands behind his back so he wouldn't yank Samara into his arms. "You made it."

"We did," Samara said. "This is my sister Frankie. Frankie, this is AJ. He owns the restaurant."

Frankie lifted her eyebrow but smiled and presented her hand to him. "Nice to meet you, AJ."

Smiling in return, he lifted her hand, much smaller and daintier than her sister's, to his lips. "Likewise, Miss Frankie." And since he had greeted one sister in such a fashion, he decided, for parity's sake, not to leave out the other. His eyes were completely focused on Samara as he kissed the back of her hand. "I'm glad you could make it."

"We were hungry," Samara said, slightly breathless.

"You're in luck, then," he murmured, drifting his thumb over the back of her hand briefly before dropping it. "I've got just the thing to satisfy."

Samara gasped while Frankie made a sound that either meant she was impressed or annoyed, but he'd turned around to lead them to the table. He pulled out chairs for both of them, though he leaned down a little too close to Samara's ear for it not to arouse suspicions in Frankie's shrewd eyes. He also determined the color of the tank top was a dark green, and he trailed his middle finger over it lightly before standing straighter. AJ grinned and winked at Frankie, and a corner of her mouth tilted up.

Perhaps he should change tactics; getting the sister on his side would make it much easier to woo Samara.

"What would you ladies like to drink?" he asked, looking first at Frankie, then Samara.

The sisters seemed to communicate with only their eyes before Samara said, "Non-carbonated water, please?"

"Excellent," he replied. "The translations for the food are on the left column, but if you have any questions, do not hesitate to ask me or any of the other servers."

"Thank you," they both said, and Samara went immediately to her menu while Frankie looked at her sister and himself before doing the same.

He went behind the bar and grabbed an unopened bottled water and two glasses. The bottle was cool in his hands, the stems of the glasses slim between his fingers. He looked over at the table again. He could only see Frankie, but given the way Samara would hide her face in the menu with great frequency, he was sure one sister was mercilessly teasing the other. He smiled.

"I see why you wanted them to have the best table, cousin."

AJ snorted and looked down at the younger and shorter man. Hazel eyes twinkled with merriment, and his curly, dark-brown hair gave him a deceptively angelic look.

"You do?" AJ asked, continuing in Greek since that was the language that had been established at the beginning of the conversation.

"Yes," he replied, looking at the table again, a grin forming on the face. "She is stunning."

"Which one?"

"The one in the black, of course."

Of course. AJ clenched his jaw and shook his head. "Not that it is really any of your business, but she is the sister of the one who has captured my interest, Spyros."

"Sisters," Spyros said, a grin forming on his face. "And how long are they in town?"

AJ shrugged, wishing his cousin would go away so he could get back to Samara.

"AJ! A customer would like to speak to you!" Anatole called.

He groaned.

"Is the water for that table?" Spyros asked.

He didn't want to, but AJ knew he would have to cede the items to his cousin. As much as he wanted to impress Samara and her sister, he didn't need his regular customers disgruntled, either.

"Behave," AJ said, putting the bottle and glasses on the bar.

"Don't I always?"

"No..."

They went in opposite directions, AJ forcing himself not to look over at Samara's table continuously. His cousin was almost as bad of a flirt as he was, but he also lacked tact. God help him if he did something to hurt Samara.

By the time he was granted his leave, AJ spotted a tray of food going over to Samara's table. He followed it and smiled slightly when he saw what the pair had chosen as appetizers.

"Boureki and Saganaki, excellent choices."

"Your cousin was most insistent," Samara said, though her smile was directed at her sister. "Seems your family's other business is flirting with foreign women."

AJ bent his mouth to her ear, making sure his breath tickled the column of her neck. "Only the foreign women we really like."

"Um...eating?" Frankie muttered, taking a bite out of her Saganaki. "This is really good."

"As with everything with the Melonakos name," AJ said, lifting his head quickly so he wouldn't give in to the urge of nipping at Samara's skin. She smelled like the orchid and her own unique scent, and he felt his body react accordingly.

Samara remained quiet, intent on her Boureki. AJ granted her a brief reprieve and asked a more benign question. "Have you ordered dinner yet?"

"Yes. Pastitsio for me and Keftedes for Frankie," Samara said, and pointed her fork to her plate. "This *is* really good."

AJ took a deep breath, realizing he couldn't say what he wanted to say with the apt and discerning audience Samara's sister provided. "I will check on your meals. Do not hesitate to call me if you need me."

Frankie's sardonic chuckle followed him into the kitchen where Spyros met him.

"Are you sure you like the one in the white?"

"Very sure. Why?"

Spyros opened his mouth and closed it, then shook his head. "She doesn't seem your type."

"My type?"

"She's short, AJ...among other things..."

"Full? Lush? An armful? Perfect for me to hold? Lovely? You've yet to tell me how she is not my type."

Spyros stepped back and held his hands in a surrender position, starting to speak, but stopped when there was a clanging of pots followed by intense Greek from behind them. AJ let the argument go; he knew better than to mediate between two prima donna chefs.

"I don't mean any offense," Spyros said after the heated fracas had calmed. "Just...her?"

"Her," AJ confirmed, seeing Frankie's and Samara's dishes were ready to go. "And you will behave."

"I want the sister anyway," Spyros grumbled.

"Good luck with that!" AJ said with a chuckle, taking the dishes from the server heading to Samara's table. "She doesn't seem to suffer fools gladly; and you, cousin, are a fool."

He left Spyros sputtering and shaking his head, bemused. Spyros was too much of a cad for him to wish on Frankie; then again, maybe a woman like Frankie was just the young lady Spyros needed to get serious about women and show them the proper respect. He reached the table, smiling automatically at Samara's easy one. This was what he was trying to prove to Samara; he respected her above all else.

"Smells heavenly," Samara said, taking a deep breath as he placed her food in front of her.

"It had to live up to you, precious," AJ said with a small wink. "Both of you," he added, placing the Keftedes in front of Frankie.

"Right..."

"You can't give me a little benefit, precious?" AJ asked with a chuckle.

"It's not my benefit you want," Frankie said back, eyeing her sister with amusement.

Samara hid her face and was entirely too focused on her food, but AJ let her be for the moment. "Not that you aren't a beautiful woman, Frankie..."

"Hey, don't have to explain to me," she said, staring at her sister. "It's about time someone noticed..."

"American men are either blind or idiots," AJ said, gazing at Samara. She was blushing and avoiding his eye contact.

"Both," Frankie said dryly. "But whatever." She took a bite of her meal and moaned. "This is so good!"

AJ inclined his head. "You ladies enjoy your meals."

He glanced his thumb along Samara's shoulder before walking away, smiling as he felt her tremble at the caress. His hand tingled deliciously, and he stared at it as he went back to the bar. He didn't get to bask in the contact for long. The evening rush started and he performed his duties as the owner of a very successful restaurant.

Twenty minutes passed before he was able to check on his personal VIPs. Their plates had already been taken away, and Samara was rubbing her belly, apparently very satisfied.

"I hope you're thinking of opening one in Philly," Samara murmured. "Or give me the recipe, somethin'!"

"That was so good!" Frankie gushed. "I almost ordered seconds, but decided to make room for dessert."

"We're both having Loukoumades," Samara informed him with a small smile. "Spyros suggested it."

AJ tried not to think about how the sound of another's man name coming from her lips irritated him, but then felt a little better it was Spyros's, someone he knew wasn't interested.

"I'm glad he was helpful," AJ said.

"Isn't that what he was supposed to be?" Frankie asked, giving him a knowing look.

"I think he's trying to get on your good side."

"Because you're not trying to do the same with Sam?"

"Frankie."

AJ shrugged, very unrepentant. "You raise a very fair point, though I'm pretty sure all of Samara's sides are good. In fact, they're perfection."

Samara bit her lip as if trying to suppress a smile.

Spyros came with their desserts, and Samara kept staring at him, even as his cousin put a plate before her. He grinned, and that seemed to snap her out of whatever trance she had been in for once again, she focused on her food. Meanwhile, he noticed Spyros bending towards Frankie, trying to finagle a date as well, but Frankie appeared cool as she pleased, merely shrugging at whatever Spyros was suggesting.

The men left the sisters alone, though Spyros was frowning a little.

AJ laughed. "She turned you down?

"She said she would go out with me if her sister went out with you."

AJ lifted his eyebrow at that. "Did she?"

"Yes. What kind of condition is that? I don't want to be around you two while trying to…"

"Trying to what?" AJ said, giving his cousin a piercing look. He was protective of Frankie, for no other reason than she was Samara's sister. He wouldn't let anyone take advantage of her—least of all his kin.

Spyros rolled his eyes and blew out a breath, the curly fringe along his forehead rising from it. "She's an adult!"

"Yes, but she is Samara's sister. You will not disrespect Frankie. Understand?"

"I don't want to disrespect her," Spyros muttered.

"Then you will behave."

"Of course!"

"Besides, your usual seduction might not work this time. Does she seem the type who is so free with her body? A man must earn her, Spyros, and that includes—and is especially—you."

"Same with you," Spyros said darkly. "Though I doubt many men have tried—"

AJ shoved his cousin against the wall beside the kitchen door. Hazel eyes went wide as they took in his angry visage. "Do not trifle with me, cousin. I love you like a brother, and I would hate to explain to Auntie why you are in the hospital with multiple broken bones.”

Spyros nodded, heeding his much taller and stronger cousin’s advice. AJ ignored the curious glances of the servers coming in and out of the kitchen and when he looked up again, he noticed another server going to Samara’s table with a leather folder in his hand. He patted Spyros on the shoulder before leaving.

“Ana,” AJ said as the server, Spyros’s sister, handed Samara the bill. “Give it to me. It’s on the house.”

“Certainly,” Ana said, giving her boss and cousin a knowing smile and leaving. He knew she was going to get more information from Spyros about their American patrons.

“You don’t have to do that,” Samara insisted, her wallet already out on the table.

AJ shook his head, placing the leather fold behind his back. “My treat, precious.”

Samara pursed her lips. “After all that food? At least let me give you a tip.”

“How about instead of a tip, you let me take you two out tomorrow if you really want to pay me back.”

Samara sighed and sat back heavily in her chair. “You are something!”

“Persistent,” AJ agreed, smiling. “I can show you and Frankie sights only us Greeks know about.”

“Would Spyros come?” Frankie asked.

“Would you like him to?”

"I don't want to be left to my own devices while you two make moon eyes at each other, so, yeah, I'd like him to come."

AJ nodded, realizing it was a fair request. "Very well. I'll meet you in front of your hotel in the morning at ten?"

"Or earlier," Frankie said with a conspiratorial gleam in her eye. "Samara is an early riser."

"Francine!"

Frankie winced. "That was unnecessary, calling out my full name like that."

AJ laughed, but he filed that information away in the back of his mind. He crouched down, squeezing the billfold with both hands so he wouldn't reach out and caress Samara's cheek as he wanted to do. "Do you have a room number I can call just in case I'm running late and I can let you know?"

Samara nodded, and he gave her the back of the receipt so she could write down the information. Her handwriting was clean with cute, small loops and large capital letters followed by tiny lowercases.

"There," she murmured, looking into his eyes.

"Thank you, precious."

"You're welcome."

She had to leave. He saw the regret creeping into her eyes and he nodded, standing, and pulling out her chair for her. Frankie beat him to it when he moved to do the same for her, but he inclined his head in acknowledgment.

"Thank you for the dinner," Frankie said.

"Yes, it was really good. The best we've had so far," Samara added.

"The best you're going to get," AJ promised, winking.

The two women rolled their eyes, and AJ chuckled. He walked them to the door, smiling to himself at how small they were compared to him. The top of Samara's head barely reached his chest. He stopped himself from pulling her into said chest and dropping a long kiss to the top of her head.

"I would walk you back," AJ said once they stepped out into the warm, Greek night. The streets were bustling and the streetlamps gave everything an amber glow. "But I have to remain here."

"We walked here fine," Samara said.

"Yes, I know," AJ whispered, approaching her and taking her hand in his. "That doesn't mean I don't wish to see you two safely back, spend more time with you, Samara."

She shivered when he said her name, and he squeezed her hand. Frankie had turned to look at passersby, giving them privacy. It was official: AJ liked Frankie very much.

"Yes," AJ said, linking his fingers through hers. His large, olive-toned hand engulfed her smaller, darker one. The sight made his male, protective streak grow. "How long are you in town?"

"Until Thursday. We have an early flight out."

It was Sunday. They had time to build something, to lay a foundation, right?

"Okay," AJ said, kissing her fingertips. "Until tomorrow. Be safe walking back."

"Are you going to call and check in on us, Dad?"

He growled playfully and pulled her to him, causing a surprised giggle to bubble forth from her. He bent his head to the ear that had the flower tucked in it, and inhaled before whispering, "The feelings I have for you are anything but paternal, *khriso mou*." He snuck in a kiss underneath the lobe, relishing in her shiver, then, reluctantly, pulled away from her.

"Have a good night," he called to both of them, his eyes completely focused on Samara.

"You too," Frankie said. Samara gave a shy nod and, upon Frankie linking arms with her, turned down the street in the direction of their hotel.

AJ remained until he couldn't see that white peasant top any longer. When he reentered his restaurant, he had a small, content smile on his face. Spyros greeted him at the host stand, looking slightly put out.

"She left without saying goodbye."

AJ chuckled. "You'll see Frankie tomorrow. We have a date. Ten, sharp."

"Ten!"

"You want to see her again, don't you?"

Spyros waved away that truth, muttering as he walked deeper into the dining area. AJ shook his head, going over seating charts with Anatole. Spyros would come; not only because he wanted to see Frankie, but also because AJ was on a mission.

And he would let no one, not even his beloved cousin, keep him from it.

THREE

It was a beautiful day in Athens. The sky was blue with big, fluffy white clouds punctuating it; the weather was mild; and the city was alive and teeming as it always was. For AJ, however, it was as if he were seeing it for the first time. Things that had become routine and unremarkable were suddenly fresh and spectacular. The Parthenon seemed much more majestic than usual; the Temple of Olympian Zeus became something significant instead of old pillars; the Temple of Hephaestus, something he passed by on the way to the restaurant every day, was suddenly worthy of stopping and observing.

All because of her.

Samara clearly loved her history and began rattling off all the Greek myths she had read as a child, recounting how fascinated she had been by them. For her to take in all the historical sites with so much awe and reverence made AJ realize just how lucky he was to have all this legacy in his backyard, to be an inheritor of such a cultural boon.

They were standing a little ways from the Temple of Hephaestus, looking down at the street below. There was complete serenity on Samara's face. Spyros and Frankie were still inside the temple, giving them a reprieve from their watchful eyes. AJ stepped behind Samara and put his hands on her shoulders, squeezing slightly.

"Have you been enjoying yourself?"

"Immensely," she replied, taking a deep breath. "This is such a gorgeous city, AJ."

"It doesn't compare to you, Samara," he murmured and squeezed her shoulders again. She smelled like mangos, and the peach sleeveless top and flowy yellow skirt she wore brought out the undertones of her brown skin. His thumbs rubbed the softness of her shoulders, and he cheered internally when she rested against him.

"Tired?"

"Not really," she whispered.

Deciding to take a risk, he moved his hands from her shoulders to come around her waist. She sucked in a breath and went rigid.

He pulled his arms away. "I'm sorry. I got caught up—"

"No, it's fine," she said, her voice breathless. "I'm just…I didn't expect it, that's all."

"I won't touch you like that if you don't want me to."

After several beats of stillness, Samara relaxed against him, bringing his arms around her waist. He closed his eyes, something inside of him understanding this was a big step for Samara, and he was humbled once again.

His fingers began to move idly over her belly. She was so soft. He loved the feel of her. He could get lost in her curves and never want to be found.

Her hand moved to cover his, and she pressed down. "AJ."

"Yes, precious?"

"Your fingers."

AJ was confused. "Yes?"

"You're tickling me."

A large grin formed on his face at her confession. He pressed her even closer to him and twirled a finger around her navel. "Oh, yes, I remember. My little Samara is ticklish, isn't she?"

"Don't even think about it!"

"Oh, I am, precious," AJ said. "But don't worry; I won't do anything right now."

She shivered, and he knew it had nothing to do with the breeze that had just picked up. "Thank you."

They remained standing there until Frankie and Spyros called out to them, then the squad made it down to Thission. Instead of going back to Melonakos, they ate at one of the small cafés in the district. It wasn't a tourist spot, but rather a local place where few, if any, of the servers spoke English. Frankie and Spyros sat across from AJ and Samara at the table. AJ put his arm on the back of Samara's seat, speaking in low tones to her while translating the menu and what was in the various dishes. This time, Samara and AJ would share the Kleftiko. Frankie remained with the tried and true Keftedes, and Spyros ordered Moussaka.

The cousins listened with amusement as the sisters said what their favorite sites had been so far and debated the pros and cons of each other's choice. AJ had dropped all pretenses of not touching Samara and wrapped his arm fully around her shoulders, his fingers drifting idly along her skin. Samara hadn't done anything to indicate she had realized his move, too engrossed in discussion with her sister. AJ paid cursory attention—laughing when appropriate, sticking up for Samara's opinion when it seemed she needed it—but was generally looking around the space to make sure everything was in order and safe. He wanted the sisters to be comfortable to fully enjoy their trip, so Samara could lower her guard. He would be all the protection and security she'd ever need, especially since she'd chosen his country to visit.

The food arrived relatively quickly considering the café was completely full. After they finished their entrees, the server asked if they wanted dessert, but all declined. Samara pulled out some bills to pay for lunch, but AJ was having none of it. He closed his hand around hers and, after a stare-down, she relented.

"Thank you," she whispered, putting her bills back into her traveler pack.

"My absolute pleasure," AJ said.

She blushed prettily, doing little to make him not want to kiss her, but he paid for the bill instead and pulled out her chair so she could stand. Immediately afterward, he took her hand in his and interlocked their fingers. She squeezed in return, though her gaze was on her sister and not him.

"Where do we want to go next?" Spyros asked once they got back on the street. Frankie had her camera out and was snapping candids. Samara shrugged.

"Do you want to go to the museums?" AJ asked. "The Agora?"

Frankie looked at them sheepishly. "I actually could go for a nap. We don't have to see the entire city in a day."

Samara chuckled and nodded. "I'm a little sleepy too. That food was *rich!*"

"We live close by," Spyros said, looking to AJ, "So you won't have to go all the way back to your hotel—"

"I don't think so," Frankie said with a frown. "We still barely know you."

"We won't hurt you, Frankie. Merely for convenience's sake. Besides, we probably should go to the restaurant for a bit anyway," AJ said, then looked to Samara. He knew Frankie would defer to whatever Samara's decision would be, and he hoped she wanted to spend as much time with him as possible, the way he wanted to spend with her.

Her eyes held her apology, and AJ knew he had lost this particular battle. Regardless that they had only known each other for not even twenty-four hours, and it was the wisest decision for two single females to make, he couldn't help but be slightly disappointed in Samara's decision.

"We should go back to the hotel."

"I understand," AJ murmured, dragging a knuckle along her cheek. "You don't feel threatened by us, though, do you?"

"No, AJ," Samara assured him. "Just for an hour, two max. You can come pick us up and we'll be refreshed for more sightseeing."

He ran his thumb over her knuckles. "Two hours."

"Gonna time us?"

"Absolutely," AJ deadpanned, though allowed the corners of his mouth to curve to show his teasing. "Bad enough I doubt I can convince you to move here permanently, yet."

She chuckled and shook her head, pulling her head from his and starting to walk in the direction they'd come. "You are so silly."

Smiling, AJ caught up with her and interlaced their fingers again. He knew she didn't understand the gravity of what had happened in the Monastiraki yesterday. He truly believed he'd met his mate in her, and maybe she was trying to reconcile that fact too. Like him, she hadn't been looking for or anticipating his arrival. Nevertheless, he liked whom he found. He hoped Samara did as well.

They took a taxi to the hotel. AJ sat in the front because of his long legs. All four got out the taxi once they arrived, though Spyros told the driver to stay since he and AJ would be returning shortly. AJ grasped Samara's chin lightly with his thumb and forefinger, once again quelling the urge to kiss her. They weren't ready for that yet.

"Until two hours," he whispered.

"Yes."

AJ's time at the restaurant kept him appropriately distracted. When he was able to check the clock again, he realized he'd gone over the allotted two hours. He whistled to Spyros to tell them they had to get to the sisters' hotel.

"I'm taking the Vespa," AJ informed Spyros on the way to their flat building. They lived across the hall from each other.

"You think Samara will like that?"

He grunted. "True. Fine. We'll take taxis and walk. I'll ask her if she would mind the scooter so tomorrow I can—"

"Whoa!" Spyros said. "Tomorrow! You plan to monopolize all her time."

"If she'll let me."

"And if she doesn't."

"I'll convince her to let me."

Spyros shook his head. "I don't know, cousin. You seem very preoccupied with this foreigner. You act as if when she leaves you won't move on to the next one after a few days."

"There is no 'next one'," AJ said, waving at one of their neighbors coming out of the flat building as they started the climb to the fourth floor. "She's The One."

"'The one' what?" Spyros asked.

He flashed his cousin a smile. "The next Mrs. Melonakos...unless you or Dimitri beat me to the altar."

Hazel eyes went wide at the declaration, and AJ winked at Spyros before unlocking the door to his flat and going inside. "Five minutes, cousin!"

AJ took the quickest shower in history and changed into a burgundy, collared, short-sleeve shirt and dark-gray slacks. He made sure he had his wallet before grabbing his leather jacket and going across the hall, knocking on Spyros's door.

"Hurry up!" he called.

A minute later, Spyros came out wearing a dark-blue, button-down shirt and brown slacks.

"You look nice," AJ said, then sniffed. "A little heavy on the cologne."

"Fuck you," Spyros said, popping his collar. "I smell divine."

Not having the time to stroke Spyros's ego, AJ rolled his eyes and hurried down the stairs, trusting his cousin would follow. He hailed a taxi and the pair went to the Marina Hotel.

AJ practically ran out the taxi once they pulled in front of the hotel, thankful Spyros had a little more sense and asked the driver to wait. When he went inside the lobby, he saw the sisters, also changed from the day's earlier attire, looking at brochures. Samara's shoulders straightened a moment before her eyes went to the entrance, spotting him there. She was wearing dark jeans that tapered at the ankles, a dark-green, Vneck, long-sleeved top, and large silver hoops in her ears.

Before he could go to her, she came to him with Frankie in tow. Frankie was also wearing straight-legged jeans, and a yellow and blue-striped long-sleeved shirt. Pearl studs were in her ears. She looked very pretty.

Yet, as usual, it was Samara who arrested all of AJ's attention.

"Hey," she said, stopping in front of him. "Thought you'd changed your mind."

"Never, *khriso mou*," AJ said and nodded at Frankie. "Hello."

"AJ," she said with a smile and led them out the hotel. Spyros glared at him, knowing the fare was growing because of the wait, but AJ didn't care.

"Do we know where we're going?" Spyros asked once they got into the taxi.

"Sis wants to see the Archaeological Museum, if that's okay," Samara said.

"Anything for you, precious," AJ said, earning one of Samara's fantastic smiles.

He paid the fare once they reached the museum, and he helped Samara out the taxi. He didn't let go of her hand once she was on her feet and she didn't try to make him. It had been a long time since he'd visited the museum; yet, he was more transfixed on Samara than the artifacts housed. Of course, he and Spyros translated the placards when asked; but for the most part, he barely paid attention.

"The art here is amazing! The sculptures..." Frankie breathed, and Samara nodded in agreement. Both he and Spyros shared a look saying the art wasn't the only thing amazing to them.

There came a point when Samara wanted to take a break, so AJ sat with her on a bench while Frankie and Spyros went off to parts unknown. He tucked her into him, and eventually she rested her head against his chest. Her eyes fell shut and he felt like someone who'd been chosen for such a treasured gift.

"Are you comfortable?"

She nodded and nuzzled him. "You make a fantastic pillow."

Pillow. Bed. He grunted—half chuckle, half groan—as his mind conjured up images of her in his bed wearing nothing but his sheets and scent.

Her arm, which was hugging him from behind, tightened, and her fingers began an idle drift. AJ trembled from her touch; but from the look of utter peace on her face, AJ knew she wasn't being coy. Despite her initial standoffishness, he was realizing she was a very affectionate person. She seemed was one of those people who loved to give contact but was too shy to receive it.

He linked fingers with her free hand, noting their different shades and her clean fingernails. She tilted up her head to look into his eyes. They were bright and clear, and she released a breathless chuckle before snuggling back into his chest. AJ held her closer. He knew she was overwhelmed, knew she saw the sincerity and probably more in his gaze. She didn't need to be shy around him, though. Any level of affection she'd like, he'd be more than happy to give.

He spotted Spyros and Frankie coming back, and he squeezed Samara's shoulder. She sat up straighter and stood.

"How was it?" Samara asked cheerily. AJ stepped behind her but didn't touch her.

Frankie hooked her arm through her sister's and started ahead. "You should've come with. It was amazing!"

They walked ahead of him and Spyros; and from their direction, he guessed they were ready to leave. When they exited the museum, AJ grasped Samara's hand again while Spyros touched Frankie's arm to get her attention.

"Where to next?" he asked.

"Food," Frankie answered.

"Dinner it shall be," Spyros said, holding out his arm. Frankie inclined her head and accepted it. AJ looked down at Samara and saw her smiling, and he squeezed her hand.

"She likes him," AJ murmured, part statement, part question.

"He's wearing her down. He's a cool person," Samara agreed.

"And I?"

"You?"

"Am I 'cool'?" AJ asked, following the younger couple, though their pace was easy.

"Seems like," she admitted. "But I'm still figuring you out."

"I'm an open book, *khriso mou*," AJ promised, lifting their joined hands to kiss her knuckles. "Anything you want to know about me, just ask."

"Really?"

"Yes."

Samara bit her lip and looked ahead of them. He suspected she had hundreds of questions whirling around, but he didn't expect her to ask anything right then, especially when Spyros and Frankie stopped at a restaurant just off Syntagma Square. As before, dinner was full of lively conversation and excellent food. This time Samara and Frankie sat side by side while the men sat across from them. AJ was having a hard time deciding if it were an improvement or a downgrade from having her next to him. At least this way, he could look at her full on, see into her deep-brown eyes and take in her gorgeous smile; spy the blush that would always creep up her cheeks whenever she noticed his intense gaze on her—which was often. However, he couldn't touch her as often as he wanted, and he wasn't a play-footsy person.

The sisters, it seemed, loved to observe people; and throughout the meal they pointed out various characters, playing "Pick out the Americans" and having fairly great success. What neither of them noticed, however, were the appreciative looks they received—especially Samara. Frankie seemed more aware of her surroundings, but she patently dismissed them, especially when Spyros began striking up a conversation with her. Samara had flashed AJ a small smile then, and started to look at the restaurant's décor.

"What are you two doing tomorrow?" he asked, eradicating their awkward lull.

Samara shrugged. "I'm not sure. I think we're going to the National Historical Museum, and then after that...winging it. Wednesday we're going to Piraeus for the day and then relaxing that night. Then Thursday we go home."

AJ's jaw clenched. He didn't want to think about Thursday. He didn't want to think about the day she would be leaving him. So instead, he focused on the days she would be here, starting with tomorrow.

"Piraeus...I have a yacht docked there."

Samara's eyes widened. "You have a *yacht*?"

AJ laughed at her shock. "It's not what you think. It's more a nice-sized boat, but nothing too fancy—an Atlantic 31. I love sailing. I've been saving up for it since I was young, and then, with a little luck in the stock market and the restaurant, as well as my father chipping in, I was able to purchase one for a deal. My father's old friend was upgrading, so he sold it to me for about a half of the market value."

"Oh, wow! That was nice of him!"

"I love it. I'm suggesting it if you don't want to wait around and buy a ticket to go on the tours. I know my way around pretty well."

She seemed excited by the prospect, and she leaned to Frankie's ear to relay the proposal to her.

"*A yacht*?!" Frankie whispered loudly. "You roll like that!"

Spyros scowled and AJ laughed, squeezing his cousin's shoulder to calm him. "It's just a boat."

Frankie sucked her teeth and shook her head. "'Just a boat.' Man, Samara...betta get on that!"

"Frankie!"

"What?" she asked unapologetically. "Not every day a fine Greek man asks you on his *yacht*!"

That blush was on Samara's cheeks again, and it got darker when AJ winked at her. She was so enchanting.

This time Spyros paid for the meal. AJ was glad their guests had learned they would pay for nothing if he and Spyros had anything to say about it, since neither sister had bothered to take out any money. It would've been the same argument over again, and AJ thought they could spend their time more fruitfully doing anything but that.

"What next?" Spyros asked, wrapping his arm around Frankie's shoulders. She rolled her eyes but didn't shrug him off, and Samara and AJ gave each other amused looks.

"What's there to do at night? We both conked out after the meal at your restaurant," Samara said with a sheepish chuckle.

"Hmm," AJ began, tapping his chin with a finger. The four of them were walking without any direction, and AJ had hooked the pinky of his right hand with the one of Samara's left hand. The night was perfect for walking and the streets were lively. "There are clubs, music festivals, outdoor cinemas..."

"Or we could always go to the Psiri, cousin," Spyros said. "There's always something to do there."

He frowned slightly. It was always so crowded there, too, but it would give them more options. Then again, crowds did give AJ an excuse to keep Samara ever-close to him.

"We follow your lead," Samara said. "You two are the natives."

"Yeah, we're flexible," Frankie added.

"Then, let's go!" Spyros exclaimed, removing his arm from Frankie's shoulders only to grab one of her hands and start walking faster, practically dragging her. Frankie laughed and told him to slow down, Samara giggling at the both of them.

"So crazy!"

"He likes to have a good time, Spyros," AJ said, bringing her closer to him. Her arm slipped through his, and they picked up the pace so they wouldn't lose the other couple.

"What goes on at the Psiri?" Samara asked.

"Lots of clubs," AJ said. "Lots of singing, eating, having of a good time. It should be fun."

Her smile was bemused. "I don't generally go to clubs in the States."

"We can always go do something else—"

"No!" Samara said, taking a deep breath. "I mean, I need to not be such a recluse. This will be good for me, going out my comfort zone."

"I don't want to put you in any uncomfortable situations, Samara," he said, stopping and looking directly into her eyes. "The minute it becomes too much, you let me know and I'll take you back to the hotel, okay?"

Her smile and eyes were soft, and she nodded. "I will."

He smiled back and squeezed her pinky with his. "Okay. Come, before they get lost in the throng."

Hands intertwined, AJ and Samara weaved their way through the crowd to find their cousin and sister and to enjoy the Athens nightlife.

FOUR

AJ had never been so hard in his life, and it was all Samara's fault.

The siren had no idea how alluring she was, and he thought that was probably part of the reason she didn't like clubs. She attracted attention, simply put, especially when she danced.

Hips shouldn't do things like that outside the bedroom...

Next to him, Spyros pressed the bottle of his beer to his forehead and fanned himself with his free hand. "Is it hot in here?"

"Scorching," AJ rasped, his eyes on the two sisters who were dancing up a storm in one of the clubs they had discovered. At first, Samara had been content on being a booth butterfly, and he'd been more than happy to let her. Far be it for him to put her up where other men could see...entice her away. He wasn't proud of his possessive streak when it came to her, but would own it nevertheless. However, this latest club they'd stumbled upon played more R&B music (Samara and Frankie called it "old school") and the sisters had been dancing nonstop ever since.

"This is my *jam!*" Samara had exclaimed when they'd first entered and had pulled Frankie to the dance floor to prove just how much she enjoyed the song playing.

AJ thought he would be content just watching and allowing the sisters to have a good time. He had hijacked all of Samara's time from the moment he'd seen her in the market. He was a big boy; he knew how to function without her by his side—

It was the other men who were growing increasingly problematic.

At first, no one had dared approach Samara and Frankie, many completely awed by the two women on the dance floor. After three songs, however, some had become bolder and decided to ask them for dances. Initially, both ladies would shake their heads; but the men were persistent, and so the women relented. AJ couldn't help but smirk when some more courageous men tried to move their hands into off-limits territory (which, for AJ, was Samara's entire body), but Samara and Frankie weren't having that. There was always space between the dancing bodies. Also, their dance partners simply couldn't keep up.

In the meantime, various ladies approached AJ for a drink, a dance, or other "activities" in the numerous dark corners of the club, but AJ politely (and sometimes not) rejected all the advances. The only woman he wanted to dance with was his American beauty.

"I'm going in," AJ muttered to Spyros in Greek after the fifth man approached Samara. He needed her in his arms before he got them thrown out and himself in jail.

Fifth Man and Samara were dancing to a song AJ didn't recognize, but it had a pulsing beat and a mean bass line that compelled Samara to shimmy her hips most enticingly. Every time Fifth Man tried to bring her closer, she would skip out of his reach so fluidly one would think it was part of the dance. AJ, however, knew otherwise, and was intent on showing all the other men just whom she preferred.

"It's me," AJ informed her as he slid one long, strong arm around Samara's waist and brought her back flush against his front, bending his legs as they dipped and swayed to the music. Fifth Man glared at him and started to say something, but the warning in AJ's eyes had him holding up his hands in surrender and leaving to find another dance partner.

Smart man.

Samara chuckled at Fifth Man's retreat. "Finally decided to get up and dance?"

"I didn't know you could move like that, *khriso mou*," AJ purred in her ear, his eyes watching Spyros turn Frankie's attention on him. Frankie smirked and went at it, a challenge in her eyes. Spyros was definitely more than up for it.

"There's a lot you don't know about me," she said.

"Going to teach me?" he murmured, inhaling her scent with his nose in the crook of her neck. Despite the height difference, it was as natural as breathing for him to do. "I can be a really good student."

Samara stopped dancing and moaned, the sound going straight to his cock and making it twitch. She tensed, no doubt having felt it against her ass, so he gave them some space.

"Come on," he encouraged, placing his hands on her hips. "Dance."

Samara was very inhibited at first, apparently still uncomfortable from their previous closeness. AJ kept his hands on her hips, guiding her movements to match his. When the second song started, her body became more fluid, and her hands roamed over the curves he'd been fascinated by from the moment he saw her.

Soon, the temptation was too much, and he began to slide his hands from her hips to her thighs. Her breath caught and her rhythm broke, but he shushed her and kissed her cheek, telling her to move. He continued to caress her, helping her get used to his touch, and soon she was moving like a goddess of the dance.

His hands changed direction and moved up her torso, but this time Samara kept moving, even arching her back to get the maximum sensation out of his touch. AJ groaned and nipped at her ear, pleased beyond measure to see her let go.

"That's it, *khriso mou*," he said, his breath heavy against her temple. "Dance for me. Move for me...let go."

Her eyes dragged closed and her lip went between her teeth. Her hands covered his, and, forgetting himself, he ground his hardness against her bum. This time, she leaned her head back and ran a hand down his arm, whispering his name. With a low growl, he spun her around, wrapping both arms around her waist and lifting her to her tiptoes, their mouths inches apart. Her eyes were wide as they stared into his, and as she licked her lips in anticipation, he could see hesitation in her gaze.

His ardor cooled. As much as he wanted to kiss her, he wouldn't do it. He wanted their first kiss unhurried and memorable, not the result of lust in a crowded, rank nightclub. He ran a single finger down her cheek and kissed the corner of her mouth. Her breath shuddered out of her, and her hands clutched his shirt.

"AJ..."

"Wanna get out of here?"

"Yeah. I'm getting a little...dizzy..."

He reluctantly let her go, and she immediately spun away from him, weaving her way through the crowd to the exit. AJ sighed and tapped on Spyros's shoulder, telling him he and Samara were stepping out for some air.

Spyros smirked at him. "I saw you, cousin," he spoke in Greek. "You're *bad*."

Frankie was also looking at him with a semi-amused, semi-concerned expression, and he squeezed her shoulder. "Come out whenever you're ready," AJ told them in English. There really was no rush.

He made it outside, taking the time to inhale a fresh, clean, proper breath. His eyes frantically searched for Samara, and he exhaled a relieved sigh when he spotted her leaning against the wall a few ways down the sidewalk. Her eyes were closed, and her hands were over her abdomen and chest. It was dangerous for her not to be aware of her surroundings, even if she did wear one of those traveler packs underneath her top.

"Samara," he called, and she opened her eyes. There was shame in them, and he shook his head and cooed at her. "Why do you look like that, precious?"

"Like what?" she asked, standing straighter and dropping her hands to her sides.

"Embarrassed. You've no reason to be embarrassed, darling."

She seemed to flush and she averted her gaze from his. "Things were getting a little, erm..."

"Hot?"

She hid her eyes with her hands and AJ chuckled, pulling them away and kissing her palms. "I feel like an idiot!"

"You are not," AJ said, shaking her hands so she would look at him. "You are a woman who feels deeply. There's nothing wrong with that."

Her expression said she didn't believe him.

"Why do you think something *is* wrong, then?" he tried, wanting to learn more about how she thought, especially about herself.

"I..." She licked her lips and looked off down the street where there was a group of drunken men singing very loudly and off-key. "I wasn't raised to be like that."

"You weren't raised to feel things deeply?"

She shrugged. "It's silly. Ignore me.

He interlocked their fingers before resting them against his chest. "I don't think it's silly. I'm not sure I understand, but I don't think you're silly. I think you're passionate, and there's nothing wrong with being passionate."

"Passion can lead me to do something incredibly out of character and unwise...and then I'll be..." She shook her head and sighed.

"What, Samara? You'll be what?"

"In trouble," she mumbled.

"What kind of trouble?"

Samara glared at him briefly before sighing. "The kind of trouble that cries and poops!"

His eyes widened. "Is that what you really think?"

She snorted. "With my luck? Yes!"

"What's your luck?"

"Murphy's law—anything that can go wrong, will!"

"Hmm...and in all the time you've known me, what, exactly, has gone wrong?"

She opened her mouth, then shut it. Groaning, Samara buried her face into his chest. AJ laughed and hugged her. Nothing had gone wrong; and if AJ had his way, nothing would.

Some minutes passed where he just held her, rubbing his hand along her back to soothe her. She relaxed fully against him, her body starting to tremble as the breeze became more pronounced.

"Here," he said, letting go of her briefly to place the jacket he wore over her shoulders. "Better?"

"Much, thanks."

They remained that way until Frankie and Spyros exited the club. Everyone was ready to go.

They all piled in the taxi, Frankie dozing against the window and Samara perilously close to joining her sister in slumber. Spyros brushed some hair from Frankie's forehead in a very tender gesture, and AJ smiled at his cousin's affectionate side. They reached the hotel far too soon for his liking, but it was nice to see the sleepy, sheepish smiles on the sisters' faces once they realized they had arrived.

"Clearly, we aren't night owls," Samara said by way of apology as AJ helped her out.

"Don't apologize. Did you have fun today?" AJ asked.

"We did, yes. Thank you."

"I'll call your room tomorrow morning okay?" AJ asked.

"Okay. Goodnight AJ, Spyros."

"Goodnight," Spyros returned.

AJ couldn't let her go away without a kiss, and he placed one upon her knuckles. "Have sweet dreams about me."

She laughed and rolled her eyes, then followed her sister into the hotel.

"That was the best time I'd had in a while," Spyros said as they went back to their flat.

AJ snickered. "And it didn't involve a bed."

"Sometimes, I *really* don't like you," Spyros groused. AJ laughed, messing Spyros's curly hair good-naturedly.

The next morning his uncle called him to the restaurant early to receive a shipment that was due there. He groaned, irritated by the reminder that he was part owner of the restaurant and had responsibilities. He called Samara's room as he got ready, telling her they would have to meet up later.

"Don't worry about us," Samara said in low tones. He assumed Frankie was still sleeping. "We'll just grab some breakfast and go to the National Historical Museum early. Might be better. Beat the crowds."

"We're going to see each other today," AJ vowed.

She laughed. "Okay, AJ. You still have a life to live, a job and all that. Don't get irresponsible for a couple of tourists."

"You're so much more than that to me, Samara," AJ said, bothered by how easily she dismissed herself.

"AJ..."

"Lunch, then? I'll call you when I'm done."

"We might not be in the hotel."

"Good point. I'll give you my mobile number."

He recited it to her, and she verified it by calling it back. Once everything was in order, he wished her a pleasant day and said he would be awaiting her call.

"You too," Samara said, and ended the call.

AJ spent the majority of the morning keeping track of the arriving crates of food and other supplies and doing some inventory. By the time he was done, it was close to two in the afternoon, and his stomach growled, reminding him he hadn't really eaten all day. He also hadn't received a call yet, or else he would've felt the phone at his hip buzz since he had it on vibrate. He checked it anyway, and was glad he hadn't, indeed, missed her call.

Inspiration struck him. He prepared an assortment of food, enough for four people, and packed a basket. He thought a picnic in the National Garden would be something new and relaxing. Spyros though it was a good idea as well, and he offered to go home quickly and get blankets for them to use. AJ was waiting in front of the restaurant for Spyros's return when his mobile finally buzzed.

"Hello," he said, hoping it was Samara.

"Hey. Samara here. We just got done; time got away from us. Are you still busy? I figured we'd call before we got something to eat."

"Perfect," AJ said, smiling and nodding to Spyros who had just returned. "Where are you now?"

"Uh..." He heard muffled conversation. "In front of the Hotel Grande Bretagne. Frankie wanted to look inside."

"Stay there. We're coming to get you."

"Now? You're done?"

"Yes. We should be there shortly. Thank you for calling, Samara."

"Of course," she replied, then ended the call.

"To the Grande," he informed Spyros, and the pair was off.

A tram ride later, the cousins walked at a brisk pace from their stop to the hotel. AJ and Spyros entered the lobby and saw the women sitting on one of the settees in the palatial space. Samara smiled at them, then frowned when she spotted the basket. She tapped Frankie on the shoulder to get her attention, and the two met up with AJ and Spyros.

"What's this?" Samara asked, pointing to the basket.

"Lunch, if you'd like," AJ said, bending down to kiss her cheek. She was wearing khaki pants and a red, scoop-neck top that fitted to her form. Frankie had on black slacks and a short-sleeved, royal blue, collared top. Both were wearing pearl earrings.

"That's nice of you," Samara said.

"And I've got blankets," Spyros said, lifting up the bag that held them.

"Awesome," Frankie said.

"Come, let's go."

They weren't in a rush to get to the park, and AJ took Samara's hand with his free one. He let Spyros choose the place, and he selected a clear patch of green not too far from a duck pond and the Zappeion. Spyros spread out the blankets while AJ set up the food; and once everything was settled, they all sat down to partake in the meal. AJ had chosen food he had seen the girls order as well as fresh grapes and strawberries to snack on. Frankie and Samara talked about what they saw in the museum while they ate, and his heart swelled when Samara announced Athens was slowly becoming one of her favorite cities.

"Can't believe we only have one full day left, though," she said sadly as they finished eating. There was still food left, but they had plenty of time to eat it.

"Yeah, I can't, either. It's like this time flew by, thanks to our tour guides," Frankie said, glancing at AJ and Spyros.

"Speaking of," Spyros said. "Want to check out the Zappeion. It's not far from here and it's a beautiful building."

"Sure," Frankie said, "Samara?"

"Nah, y'all go on ahead," Samara murmured, pointedly not looking at AJ. Frankie gave them a knowing smirk, but nodded. "All right. Be back in a while."

Spyros helped Frankie to her feet and, after grabbing some food to feed to the ducks, went off toward the Zappeion. AJ, who'd been lying on his side, reached his hand to touch Samara's.

"You didn't want to go?" Samara asked.

"All I want to see and explore is right here," he said softly, drifting his thumb along her the lines in her palm.

She sighed and closed her fingers over his thumb. "The things you say, AJ...you say it to all the foreign women you meet?"

He wouldn't lie to her. "I've been known to say them from time to time."

"Did you mean them?"

"Yes, for that period of time, I did."

Samara nodded. "Okay. Thank you for being honest with me."

AJ didn't like her despondent tone, and he sat up. He tugged her hand to get her attention. "Hey."

Samara granted it to him. "Yes?"

"Those were all practice runs for the times I would mean it, precious," he said clearly, so she wouldn't misunderstand. "I've been nothing but sincere and genuine with you."

She looked at him skeptically and scoffed. "Even when you call me precious?"

"*Especially* then!" She seemed taken aback by his adamancy, and he tugged her hand again. "Come here." He patted the space between his legs.

She looked at him shyly and he smiled, tugging on her hand once more. She finally moved; and once she was between his legs, his arms wrapped around her tightly and his legs enveloped hers.

"Samara, you are precious...so precious. When I first saw you, I felt awed. You were stunning from afar, and the fact your personality matches your outer beauty only makes you even more beautiful in my eyes. Please believe me, *khriso mou.*"

She said nothing and bowed her head. A few seconds later, he heard her sniffle.

"Did I say something wrong?" AJ asked, panic coloring his voice.

"The opposite," she said wetly, trying to wipe away her cheeks quickly. "God, I didn't expect to feel all of this after hearing that. I'm sorry."

"Shh," AJ intoned with understanding and pulled her to his chest, telling her to let it out. He rocked her as she wept, brushing away her tears as he sang softly in Greek. Though he knew she didn't understand what he was saying, he knew she appreciated his efforts by the way she snuggled deeper into him.

"I'm sorry," she apologized again after she calmed. "I'm just...I'm so overwhelmed."

"I am too," AJ admitted, unable to hide his tremors from her gently stroking his chest. "I can't believe I finally found you."

"Found me?"

"Yes," he whispered against her temple. "God, you feel so perfect in my arms." He held her tighter, and a few minutes passed without either of them speaking.

"I like being held by you," Samara confessed quietly. "You make me feel so cherished."

"Because you are," AJ said, tilting up her chin to look into her eyes. "You are very cherished." His thumb brushed her lips, and he felt them quiver. Samara tucked her head underneath his chin, and after a few moments, began to doze.

He gazed at her while she slept, wondered if she dreamed. She deserved nothing but pleasant ones, and if he could do anything to help her get them, he would. Eventually, he lay back, keeping her on top of him for her to use him as a pillow. She woke up thirty minutes later, and he grinned at her sheepish look.

"Hello, gorgeous. Sleep well?"

"I'm sorry," she said. "I didn't mean to fall asleep."

"That's the ultimate trust, you know, falling asleep with someone."

"Is it?"

"I'd think so."

"I have to trust you on that, seeing as I've never done it before."

He raised his eyebrows at that, surprised by the admission, but he was also smug. Smiling gently, he kissed her fingers. "Thank you for allowing me the honor of being your first," he murmured against her knuckles.

She chuckled and rolled her eyes before sitting up. "What time is it? Should Frankie and Spyros be back yet?"

AJ shrugged and shifted so he rested his head in her lap. She let out a startled laugh, and he gave her a devilish grin and wink. "Much better."

"Really?"

"What?" he asked, closing his eyes and nuzzling his face in her belly.

"AJ!"

"So soft," he murmured, and pouted when she pushed his face away. "What?"

"No way!"

"'No way' what?"

"What you need to be all up in my tummy for?"

"I like it," AJ said, but frowned upon seeing embarrassment and shame in her eyes. "Precious..." He sat up. She looked away, her bottom lip trembling.

"What's wrong?" he asked quietly.

"You're touching me," she whispered.

"Trying to, yes," he said with a slight smile.

"But you're touching me like you *want* to."

"I do," AJ said seriously, frowning. "This isn't common practice in America?"

Samara snorted, her laugh brittle and lifeless. "My butt, yes. My boobs, definitely. My stomach? No, men don't really like that part of me."

"All of you is beautiful," AJ said quietly. "I've had a hell of a time trying to keep my hands in respectable places as it is."

Her cheeks reddened even as a smile stretched her lips. "AJ."

"Seriously," he said, smiling a little. "You are a delight that I want to savor." Pursing his lips, he lay his head back in her lap and took her hand in his. He then placed her palm on top of his flat stomach. "See? How's that?"

She shook her head, but kept her hand exactly where he had placed it. "It's not the same and you know it."

AJ shrugged. "Maybe not, but if you've not been touched much, you probably haven't done much touching, either, right?"

Her lips flattened but she gave a jerky nod.

"Okay," he said, patting the back of her hand. "I'm more comfortable with it, so...touch me, Samara. Explore me."

Her touch was timid and fleeting at first, so he took his hand and used it to guide hers along his stomach, his abdominal muscles, even higher. He watched her face as she studied her hand upon his torso. When she brushed her fingers against his nipple, he groaned.

"I'm sorry," she said, about to snatch her hand away, but he kept it in place.

"Don't apologize," he breathed, "I love your touch."

"Oh. Okay." She allowed her fingers to graze his nipple again, and he took a deep breath. She moved to his other pectoral and fully cupped it, and he bit back another groan.

"Do you work out?" she asked.

"Not regularly," AJ said. "Or at least, not traditionally. I do a lot of moving at the restaurant, a lot of lifting. And I have free weights at home, but they mostly collect dust."

"Well, you feel very fit," she said, her eyes darting to his before going back to his torso. "You're very defined."

Her tone wasn't seductive in the least, very matter-of-fact, as if she were going down a checklist. He took her hand and rested their clasped hands against his heart.

"Have dinner with me tonight. Just the two of us."

She frowned. "But what about Frankie?"

"I think she'll be all right," AJ said. "And if she wants a partner, Spyros can be a gentleman when he wants to be."

Samara shook her head. "It would be rude of me. We came together on vacation. I'm supposed to look out for her."

"And yet, for the better part of an hour, you've been here alone with me."

She dropped her head. "I have. Perhaps I should've gone with—"

"You're afraid," AJ said, squeezing her hand. "Why?"

She shook her head and tried to pull her hand away, but he wouldn't let her. AJ thought she was using her sister as a smokescreen and he wouldn't let her, especially not when they were on borrowed time. Frankie could handle herself.

"Sam—"

"I have to set an example for her," Samara interrupted. "What would it look like if I go off with a stranger?"

"Do I feel like a stranger to you?" AJ asked, irritation growing. "We've been together for the past three days. In all that time, you've never felt like a stranger to me. So, have I felt like a stranger to you?"

After a pause, Samara shook her head.

"So why are you afraid, Samara? You know I won't hurt you. And you said yourself you weren't threatened by me—"

"You make me *feel*," Samara croaked. "You..." She shook her head again and licked her lips.

AJ sat up at that and brought his face to hers so she had no choice but to look into his eyes. "Are they scary feelings?"

"Yes!"

"Good scary or bad scary?"

"*Scary* scary! I don't know what to do! I don't know how to act around you! You intimidate me, and I feel like an idiot!"

There was raw pain in her voice, and his heart broke for her. Samara had been hurt. It went deep and was still unhealed. He leaned his forehead against hers, their noses touching, their breaths mingling. He cupped her jaw and ran his thumb over her cheek.

"I don't think you're an idiot, Samara," he said sincerely. "What can I do to make you comfortable, *khriso mou*? The last thing I want you to be is scared or unsure. If you'd like, I can leave and never see you again if that would make things better."

"It won't," Samara whispered. She clenched her hands into fists in her lap.

"Then what can I do? What do you want to do?"

"I don't know. But I don't want to...miss you..."

FIVE

Spyros and Frankie returned, leaving AJ and Samara unable to finish the conversation. Samara started packing up the food and Spyros helped her fold the blanket. AJ took that opportunity to pull Frankie aside so he could talk to her.

"How was the Zappeion?" he asked as an opener.

"Fine. It's pretty."

"Yes."

"And what did y'all do?"

"Talk."

"That's it?"

"What else did you think would happen?" Frankie shrugged.

AJ frowned at her, not liking her body language. "Do you have a problem with me, Frankie?"

She shrugged again. "I don't know you well enough to have a problem with you."

There was a bite to her voice, and AJ nodded. "Meaning, Samara doesn't know me well enough to..." He let the sentence hang.

"Spyros said you're usually pretty friendly with foreign women."

"He did." It wasn't a question.

"He also said you've never been friendly with someone like Samara."

"I've never met anyone like Samara," he said carefully, wondering if he should be angry at his cousin yet.

"So why my sister?"

"Why your sister?"

"Why are you interested in her if she's not your type?"

AJ cut his eyes to Samara and his cousin, noticing how much more relaxed she seemed to be with him. She wasn't intimidated by Spyros because she didn't like Spyros; and perhaps more importantly, he wasn't interested in her.

"Why is your sister so shy?"

Frankie shrugged. "I don't know."

"Was she like this with other men?"

Frankie glared at him. "How is that any of your business?"

His frustration growing, AJ released a deep breath to expel it. "I really like your sister, Frankie. I just want to make sure I don't do or say anything that would upset her."

She looked at him for a long moment, then closed her eyes. "There've never been other men."

He blinked. Surely, he hadn't heard right. "I'm sorry?"

Frankie glared at him. "You heard me."

He sputtered. "B-but why? What's wrong with the men in your country?"

"I've never had a boyfriend, either," Frankie muttered and scowled. "Samara says I intimidate men."

AJ chuckled incredulously. "You don't think so?"

"How am I gonna intimidate anyone?"

"I'm intimidated just talking to you," AJ admitted.

She smiled slowly. "Really?"

"Yes. You are straight to the point, don't like games. We men, Frankie, we love games."

"Exactly. So why should I trust you with Samara?"

Frankie was sharp. She would certainly keep him on his toes. "You should trust me with Samara because she is my heart, and she is the last person I want to hurt or break. I want to show her who a true man is, and I'll strive every day to be deserving of her."

"You mean tomorrow? That's the only day you've got!"

Again, another reminder of their godforsaken deadline. "I don't plan for our relationship to end on Thursday, Frankie."

"So y'all in a relationship now?"

"Yes."

Frankie quirked an eyebrow but didn't challenge that statement. AJ wouldn't retract it, either. He and Samara had been building upon that first connection in the market, and it wouldn't end just because she lived across the Atlantic.

"What does AJ stand for?" Frankie asked, interrupting his musings.

"Alejandro. My name is Alejandro Kyriakos Melonakos."

"Alejandro? That's not Greek, is it?"

He smiled. "Spanish. My mother's from Seville."

"How old are you?"

"Thirty-four."

"Samara's twenty-four. You're a lot older than she is."

"She's an adult."

"With the experience of someone half her age!"

"Wait a minute, just *who* is the older sister, here?"

"Look," Frankie said, rolling her eyes, but there was a tiny smile on her face. "She looks out for me, and I look out for her. You're thirty-four and have loads of experience. You could take advantage of her if you wanted. I'm trying to make sure you won't."

"And how could you stop me, even if I had any intentions of hurting her, which I don't."

"We're a family of lawyers, Mr. Melonakos. Trust me; you don't want to cross us."

"Thanks for the advice."

Samara and Spyros came toward them with Samara's curious eyes darting between them. "Everything okay?"

"Possibly," Frankie said cryptically, eyeing AJ.

"Yes," AJ answered, reaching out and taking Samara's hand. "And things will be even better once you agree to have dinner with me tonight."

Samara sighed. "I told you I can't. I'm with Frankie."

"Wait. Do you *want* to go to dinner?" Frankie asked, shifting her attention from AJ to her sister.

Samara was careful not to look at AJ, perhaps knowing he would see the truth in her eyes. "Doesn't matter whether I want to or not. We're here together, and I don't want to leave you hanging like that."

"I..." Frankie began, looking at AJ suspiciously before trying again. "Samara, do you want to have dinner with AJ?"

Samara bit her lip, and AJ squeezed her hand to offer his support. "Frankie—"

"Yes or no question, Sam."

Samara glanced at him and nodded.

"Okay," Frankie said, approaching AJ. "I want all your contact information just in case I need to get in touch with you. Not just your mobile."

Samara gasped and AJ smile at Frankie's permission. "I'll do you one better. You can come visit and check out the place, and I'll give you the information there."

Frankie arched an eyebrow. "Suck up."

"If I have to be," AJ said unapologetically, squeezing Samara's hand once more before they left the park and went to AJ's flat.

"Here we are," AJ said, opening his flat's door and telling them to go in before him. It wasn't big, but there were two bedrooms, a nice-sized living area, and an eat-in kitchen. The floors were hardwood with Turkish rugs to soften up the place. His furniture was leather and burgundy red with a dark wood coffee table in front of the couch. He had a top-of-the-line entertainment system as well as nautical maps and barometers on his wall that he checked just before deciding to go to the marina. On his bookcase stood many diverse tomes and his diploma from the University of Athens.

"What did you study?" Frankie asked.

"Economics. Then I moved to London and worked in the financial district there for about seven years before growing bored and moving back home," AJ said. "I still have an investment portfolio, however, and it's doing quite well."

Frankie nodded, seeming pleased with the answer. Samara nodded as well. "It's a beautiful place. All I have is a studio, but I love it."

"What do you do?" AJ asked, realizing he really had no idea what she did for a living.

"I've been doing paralegal work at my family's law offices in Philadelphia."

"Do you want to be a lawyer?" AJ asked, remembering what Frankie said about their family and lawyers.

"I still haven't decided, actually!" Samara laughed. "Right now, I'm happy with what I'm doing, so I'm not overly pressed."

"Do you want to see my flat, Frankie?" Spyros's voice cut through their conversation. "It's just across the hall."

Frankie and Samara shared a look before the younger woman shrugged and nodded. Samara was about to follow, but AJ tugged her back to him.

"I think I should check out his apartment," Samara said, though she pressed her chest against his.

"She'll be fine," AJ murmured, squeezing her hand. "Trust her."

"I do, it's just..."

"Come on, Samara," AJ said, shaking her hand tenderly. "Trust me. Trust *yourself*, your instincts. Do you feel unsafe?"

She shook her head.

"Uncomfortable?"

She nodded.

"Good or bad uncomfortable?"

"Is there a difference?"

"You know there is," AJ said, smiling at her. "What do you want for dinner, love?"

"I don't care," Samara said dazedly. There was a tiny, shy smile on her face, and soon she wrapped her arms around his waist and dropped her forehead to his chest. They remained that way until Spyros entered the flat with Frankie in tow. Samara pulled away and had a quiet conference with Frankie while Spyros approached him.

"I gave her our information," Spyros told him. "Samara's getting a copy of it too—Frankie insisted."

AJ laughed a little. "Why do you sound put out by that?"

"I've never met such cautious girls in my life!"

"They're traveling alone, and they're inexperienced. How can you blame them for that?"

Spyros sighed and conceded his point, then his eyes turned wicked. "You plan on turning this into a sleepover?"

AJ's eyes went dark. "That's none of your business."

Spyros pouted a little. "Well! You usually have no problem telling—" He stopped talking and his eyes went wide. "You're *serious* about this one!"

"Just caught on to that?" AJ asked sarcastically.

"But...*three days*, AJ?"

"Hey, remember Dimitri's friend, Tyson?" AJ said, referencing their American cousin's Navy SEAL team member. "He met and married his wife in the span of twelve hours!"

"Oh, you're a right tortoise then!" Spyros muttered, rolling his eyes.

"They're still together and very happy," AJ continued, ignoring his cousin's cheek.

"But that's them and this is you. They're also from the same country. Just be careful. She's not the only inexperienced one in this relationship, you know."

AJ was so stunned by Spyros's insight that he completely missed his cousin and Frankie telling them goodbye. Though he wasn't inexperienced in the strictest sense, he was new to the feelings inside of him, and the fact Spyros recognized that made AJ feel self-conscious for the first time in a long while. It wasn't until he heard the door close and saw Samara leaning against it that AJ returned to the present. She stared at him, looked to him for guidance, and he offered her a gentle smile, holding out his hand to her.

"Come to me, precious."

She bit her lip and complied; and as soon as her fingers grasped his, he pulled her to him for another embrace. He cupped the back of her head and held her tightly, closing his eyes and letting the feelings she evoked run through him. He'd never been in love before, not like this, and it was obvious to everyone except for the one person who needed to see it most. Then again, Samara didn't know what she was looking for, and AJ decided he would show her.

"Are you very hungry?" he murmured, not wanting to break the spell they were under.

"Not really," she replied just as quietly, pressing closer to him. She began nuzzling his chest and he smiled.

"You like holding me, precious?" She nodded. "Would you just like to do that, then? We can sit on the couch and cuddle."

"Okay."

AJ separated from her so he could put on some music. Traditional Greek melodies filtered through the room. She was already on the couch, her posture a little rigid, and he stood in front of her. "Would you like something to drink? Water? Wine?"

"Water, please. I don't drink."

"Really?"

"I don't like the taste," she said with a small scowl.

AJ grinned. "Would you like to taste Greek wine? Lysimelis? It's similar to Merlot, but I think it is sweeter. Do you like sweet things, Samara?"

She laughed and nodded. "Trying to get me drunk?"

"No," said AJ, crouching before her and cupping her cheek. "I want you in control of all your faculties, *khriso mou*. I don't want you to forget this night or regret it, but wine might relax you, okay? Just a taste."

"All right."

Going into his kitchen, AJ pulled down two glasses and filled one with water and left the other unfilled as he used one hand to hold the empty glass and wine bottle while the other hand held the water. He set the items on his coffee table before going back to the kitchen and taking some snacks from the basket that remained from their picnic.

"Here we are," he said, putting the items next to the previous ones, and he earned Samara's smile. "I'll get the wine opener and then I'll be ready to join you."

"No rush," Samara said, but he disagreed. He was in a hurry to spend alone time with her, and had been for the past three days.

He finally returned and sat next to Samara, their thighs brushing as he settled on the edge of the couch and opened the bottle. He poured the wine half-full in the glass and then presented it to Samara.

"Have a taste," he said lowly.

Samara put down the glass of water she had just sipped from and took AJ's glass. Her nose scrunched up as she took in the aroma, and then she tipped back the glass for a taste. She licked her lips as she pulled the glass from her mouth.

"Well?"

"Not bad," Samara conceded, then took another sip as if to confirm her judgment. "Yeah, not bad. I'm not used to wine, but that's not bad at all."

"We can get you a bottle tomorrow," AJ promised. "I'm glad you liked it."

"Thank you," she said, handing the glass back to him. AJ plucked a grape and held it up to her mouth. "What are you doing?"

"You don't want?" AJ asked, rubbing the fruit against her lips. Samara's eyelids fluttered, and then she opened her mouth. AJ made sure his fingers followed the grape between her lips, and he stroked her tongue briefly before pulling out his fingers and placing them into his own mouth.

"So sweet. I wonder if that's you or the wine," he said, his eyes intense on her.

Samara's breath caught, and he watched her swallow the grape before responding. "The wine."

"I don't think so," AJ said. "What I tasted was much sweeter than the wine."

Samara grinned and punched his shoulder lightly. "You are such a flirt!"

"Am I?" AJ asked, abandoning the wine and grapes in favor of setting his lips to her neck. Samara gasped and jerked, and he placed his hand on her belly to calm her. "I'm tasting you now, Samara. You're much sweeter, *khriso mou.*"

"AJ..."

"The sweetest thing," he insisted, his mouth going from the underside of her jaw to her cheek. He moved his hand from her belly to cup her face. Her eyes were wide and luminous as he looked into them.

"Samara, precious," AJ whispered.

"Yes?"

"What is your last name?"

Samara frowned and blinked, clearly not expecting that. "Huh?"

He grinned and caressed her bottom lip with his thumb. "Your last name. What is it?"

"Grossman."

"Samara Grossman," he said. "You are the sweetest thing I've ever tasted." He brushed her lips with the pad of his thumb again. "May I have another?"

"Another what?"

"Taste."

Her nod was all but imperceptible, but she didn't pull away from him. Giving her a tiny smile, he kissed her cheek, then moved his lips to the corner of her mouth. Samara sighed, her eyes drifting closed, and it was at that moment that he placed his mouth atop hers.

Her lips were moist and full, and they trembled underneath his. His hand on her face caressed, trying to soothe her nerves. Her breath was harsh from her nostrils and fanned against his upper lip, and he pulled away from her slowly.

"Are you okay?" he asked.

"Was I?"

That response didn't make much sense and he frowned a little. "When was the last time you were kissed, precious?"

She blinked. "Freshman year in college."

He stroked her cheek in understanding. "Would you feel more comfortable if you kissed me?"

"No."

"Why?"

"I told you, you intimidate me."

AJ hummed low in his throat. "I see." He slid off the couch and situated himself between her legs on the floor. Samara laughed as he wiggled his back against the couch and her legs, nuzzling his cheek against her knee.

"What are you doing?"

"Not intimidating you," AJ said.

She laughed. "By sitting on the floor!"

He tilted his head back to rest against her stomach, his hands sliding up and down her shins. "If this makes you more comfortable, then yes," he said, and he gave her a wink.

"But how is it supposed to make me more comfortable?"

AJ shrugged. "Well, I'm on the floor, and you're on the couch. You have the upper hand, so to speak. I'm at your mercy, precious. Feel free to do whatever you want. No rush."

He picked up her hands and put them on his chest, then waited, letting her take it from there. She didn't move her hands immediately, but her fingers sent tiny pulses into his chest. AJ closed his eyes and relaxed, especially when her touch moved from his chest to his hair. Her strokes were unhurried, and she applied the perfect pressure.

"Mmm, precious, that feels wonderful."

"Good. I've...actually wanted to do this for a while."

"Really?"

"Yes. I've always wanted to run my fingers through a guy's hair."

"Whenever you want, baby, you can. I love your touch," AJ said, turning to kiss her knee. He smiled as he felt her buss the top of his head. Progress.

"You're an affectionate girl, aren't you?"

"Says you. My family acts like it's a big deal when I hug them."

"Hmm. Is it?"

"What?"

"A big deal."

"I guess. My family isn't all that affectionate in the first place, so I don't understand the critique."

"You should be how you are," he said.

A stretch of silence. "I am."

"You deserve to be happy too. You deserve to meet *your* expectations."

"I know."

"Then why do you sound so doubtful, precious?"

She took a deep breath. "I don't want to come across as selfish."

He nodded and turned to her, sitting on his knees. He put his face to hers; and if he leaned forward a centimeter more, he would be kissing her. "Fine. I expect you to be happy and selfish. With me. Think you can do that?"

Samara laughed. "I'll do my best."

"Okay. Then kiss me, Samara."

"I'm sorely out of practice, you know."

"Then I'll teach you. But I want you to kiss me. That would make me happy, Samara, and I'll bet it would make you happy too."

She licked her lips, and it was all he could do not to kiss her himself. He remained where he was though, between her legs, hands braced on the outsides of her thighs. He wanted her to take the initiative, to be in control. He wanted her to build confidence.

Her lips were fleeting against his, just a tiny peck, and he balled his hands into fists so he wouldn't pull her in for a harder, longer kiss. He touched his nose to hers in silent encouragement for more, and she obliged.

This kiss was firmer, still closed-mouthed, but it was something. It also lasted longer, and two seconds later she was pulling back and looking at him, trying to gauge his approval.

He smiled at her. "I'm happy, Samara. Are you happy?"

Her smile matched his. "Yes."

"Did you enjoy kissing me?"

"Yes."

"You can touch me when you kiss me. You don't have to have your hands in your lap." So saying, he placed one on his shoulder and the other on his cheek. "Kiss me again, precious. Be freer."

Her lips surrounded his bottom one, and the thumb on his cheek began a tentative caress. AJ groaned low in his throat, and she answered it with a moan. That compelled him to wrap an arm around her waist and bring her closer, and he opened her mouth and touched her teeth with his tongue.

Samara sighed but went along with it, opening her mouth wider so their tongues could meet. At first contact, she shied away, so he retreated and nipped her bottom lip between his teeth.

"AJ..." She sighed and pressed her tongue to his upper lip.

He groaned louder and surged his tongue inside her mouth. Her fingers tangled in his hair and he pressed her against the couch, encouraging her to wrap her legs around his waist. He could smell her feminine musk, and he was instantly harder than a diamond.

"Your body is ready for me, Samara," AJ said, dragging his mouth from hers to nibble at her jaw and neck.

"Oh..."

"I can smell you, precious," he said against her collarbone, then put his hand between her legs. She bucked and groaned. "I can feel you."

"AJ, please."

"How many men have touched you here, Samara?"

"Two."

"Two? Did they make you come, Samara?"

"No."

He moved his mouth down her sternum and began to undo her pants. She braced her hands on his shoulders, squeezing almost painfully. He nipped at her skin as he slid his hand underneath her pants and panties, feeling her unshaven mound and below. Her nubbin was hard, large, and wet, and he teased it.

"Do you think the third time is the charm, Samara?" She whimpered. "Think I can make you come?"

"Yes..."

"What was that, *khriso mou?*"

"Yes!"

Not one to disappoint a lady, he darted his fingers along her knot and into the moist crevice below it. She felt like heaven. He pulled back and watched her, brown skin flushed, beads of sweat along her hairline, soundless gasps from her mouth as her hips bucked in time with his fingers. She bit her lip and her breath caught, and then suddenly she flooded his hand with her essence. He used his other hand to caress her stomach and soothe her, her body shuddering every now and again in the aftermath. He had never witnessed anything so beautiful.

He kissed her sweetly. "Are you all right?"

She nodded.

He couldn't help but tease her, flashing a wicked grin. "Seems I can make you very happy, Samara."

Her answering laugh was music to his ears.

Six

They decided on Greek pizza for dinner. AJ gave her some privacy to clean up while he called to order it from Melonakos. He'd set out some more comfortable clothes for her in the meantime, wanting her to be as relaxed as possible. He'd feared they might be too big, but she'd snorted and said they would fit.

He washed his hands in the kitchen and pulled down dishes, opting for the living area instead of the impersonal dining table. He also lit two candles and refilled the glasses with wine and water. He was just standing straighter when Samara came out wearing an old University of Athens sweatshirt and his boxers. She was practically swimming in them.

He smiled widely. "You are so adorable."

Samara giggled and approached him, closing her eyes as his hands framed her beautiful face. He kissed her lips lightly, and when he pulled away, her face wore a tiny smile. AJ merely stared at her, taking in her beauty and serenity. He then looked around his kitchen, his flat, and noted how much more of a *home* it felt now that Samara was inside of it. When he felt her touch on his cheeks, he redirected his attention to her.

"Yes, my love?"

She blinked at him, then tucked her head into his chest. "Never mind."

He was curious. "Are you sure?"

"Yes. It was unimportant."

"*Khriso mou*, nothing you could ever think would be unimportant."

A few minutes later, the doorbell rang, and they separated. AJ opened the door and took the pizza from Anatole. His teenaged cousin was nosy and tried to look around AJ to spy Samara, but AJ gave him a hard look and a clipped, "Thank you", making sure Anatole got the hint.

He winked as he left, and AJ rolled his eyes. Cads. His cousins could be a bunch of cads.

"That smells good," Samara said.

"I hope it is to your liking," AJ replied, placing the box on the coffee table and opening it. The pizza exploded with feta cheese, tomato, spinach, and ham, and the crust was large and thick. They settled on the floor in front of his coffee table, he resting his back against the couch and setting her between his legs in front of him. He took the first slice and held it to her mouth, earning another giggle and her compliance.

"How is it, precious?" he asked before taking a bite of the same slice.

"Wow, I normally don't like tomato, but I can make an exception for this!" she said, pulling her own slice of the pie and taking a hearty bite. For the next fifteen minutes they ate, commenting on the quality of Melonakos culinary arts and AJ swiping prominent toppings from Samara's pizza slices. She would give indignant gasps and pop his knee, but that only made him laugh and nuzzle her neck in response. There was still a third of a pie left when both had decided they'd had their fill.

Neither moved. They let the food digest in their stomachs and AJ cradled Samara to his chest. He looked down upon her clear, peaceful face, her eyes closed and the tiniest of smiles on her lips. AJ began and nuzzling the curve of her neck.

"Are you happy, Samara?" he asked, his voice riding just under the music that was still playing.

"You fed me. How can I not be?"

AJ chuckled and held her tighter. His lips pressed against her jawline, and Samara smiled more. He could easily see himself doing this with her every night. Maybe next time there would be pasta, more lamb, maybe even an American hamburger if she liked. After dinner in the living area, they would cuddle just like this, not saying anything but enjoying each other's presence, until that moment when it was time to go to bed.

And cuddle more.

Or...other...activities...

AJ remembered her tightness around his fingers and almost groaned. His Samara was untouched, the two bumbling idiots she'd experimented with before be damned. They clearly weren't worthy of the title "men" if they couldn't make this passionate woman experience the highest pleasure. He'd barely touched her, explored her, and she'd shattered so wonderfully. He wanted to see how else he could make her explode.

"Are you all right?"

Samara's sweet voice brought him back to the present, and AJ kissed her temple. "I'm perfect. I'm with you, after all."

She snuggled deeper into him and chuckled. "You are so full of it."

"Full of what?"

Samara shook her head and didn't answer. She grabbed one of his hands and splayed her palm against his. He linked their fingers together, noting the differences in their sizes and shades and thinking them thrilling in their beauty. He used his other hand to trail a finger over each of hers.

"You're very affectionate," Samara murmured.

"Am I?" AJ asked, pressing his cheek against hers.

"Yes. Is that a European thing?"

"Maybe that's part of it. But it's mostly I can't be near you and not touch you. Does it bother you?"

Samara rubbed her cheek against his, and he wondered if she minded his goatee.

"No. It's nice."

Samara leaned her head against his shoulder so she could look at him. He trailed a finger down the bridge of her nose and over her soft lips. He bent his head and replaced his finger with his mouth, cupping her cheek so he could kiss her fully.

"You don't have to worry about anything, my Samara," he murmured as he broke the kiss.

Samara smiled. He adored her so much.

A knock on the door made them jump. Frowning, AJ pressed a kiss to her temple and told her to stay while he went to see who was at the door. When he saw, he let out a chuckle and spoke in Greek.

"One moment. I need to get my wallet."

He winked at Samara, who was looking at the door with a curious expression. AJ retrieved his wallet from the nightstand in his bedroom and returned to the door. He paid the deliveryman and took the large package from him. With a final goodbye, AJ closed the door and leaned against it, showing Samara what he just received.

"What is it?" she asked with a curious grin.

"You want to see the painting?"

Her eyes went wide, and she nodded, scrambling to her feet. AJ led them into his bedroom where he tore off the brown paper that covered the art. When the framed painting was revealed, both let out a gasp of awe.

"Oh, my," Samara breathed. "Oh, wow!"

Even though he had seen it before, he was just as breathless as Samara. The painter had a hell of a lot more talent than one should have when painting for pennies and tourists. Or maybe it was just he and Samara who'd inspired the masterpiece before them. It was as if the artist had seen the love before they did themselves and had captured it on canvas. AJ thought back to what the artist had said, about him and Samara being in love. Could people fall in love in an hour? Deep enough for strangers to see?

Tears fell down her cheeks as she gazed at the art. Concerned, AJ lifted her face to his and used a gentle thumb to wipe away her tears.

"Samara?"

"You..." she began, then shook her head and looked back at the painting. "I never..."

"You never what, *khriso mou?*"

"That look...you only see that look in movies."

"That look?" AJ repeated, staring at the painting in confusion.

Samara licked her lips and glanced at him helplessly. "It's only been three days...that painting..."

AJ caught on, and he smiled despite the hammering his heart was doing inside his chest. "He gave us the painting for free because of that look, Samara. What he captured in that painting...it's as rare as it is pure. And it's true. Dear God, Samara...it's so true."

She closed her eyes and two more tears trailed down her cheeks, AJ brushing them away with careful fingers. She looked back at him with her deep-brown eyes, and her hand came up to his cheek. It was the first time she had touched him on her own volition, and he closed his eyes at the contact.

"I never saw his face," she said softly. "My dream man. He was always a shadow, a cloud. Who knew he would be you?"

AJ kissed her palm again, then placed it over his heart. "This belongs to you, sweet Samara. It's completely and totally yours."

AJ pulled her close and held her. He exhaled slowly, and Samara tightened her arms around him. When he had gone into the market, the last thing he had expected to find was his complement. His wife. The mother of his children. The person who owned his heart. The person whose heart belonged to him in return.

"May we lie together, Samara?" he asked quietly. "May I hold you?"

She nodded and kissed his chest. "Yes."

AJ pulled down the covers and settled her between them. He then propped the painting against the wall carefully before changing into his pajama bottoms and joining her. They lay on their sides facing each other, their hands and fingers exploratory. They continued until their eyes drifted closed.

The blaring ring of a phone startled AJ. He looked down to see Samara sleeping, snuggled into his side. He looked behind him to his other nightstand to see the time.

Eleven at night.

He cursed, more at the fact the phone was being a loud nuisance than at the fact the time had gotten away from them, and he reached over his love's sleeping form to answer the phone.

"What?" he all but growled into the receiver in Greek.

"AJ?"

His tone considerably softened. "Oh, Frankie. I apologize."

"Is Samara still with you?"

"Yes, why?"

Frankie blew out a breath. "Okay, good. I was calling to make sure. I'd just gotten back and I didn't see her here."

"Are you okay, Frankie?"

"I'm fine. Spyros and I went back to the Psiri, and then we saw a movie in one of the gardens. It was really nice."

"How nice?" AJ couldn't help but tease.

Frankie sucked her teeth. "That is none of your business! Can I speak to Samara?"

"She's sleeping."

"Wore her out, huh?"

AJ blushed but affected a gasp. "Now who is trying to pry in business that doesn't belong to her?"

Frankie huffed, but chuckled. "Fine. I'll get the dish anyway. Is she coming back to the hotel?"

"No."

"I figured as much." Frankie sighed. "It's late, and she won't be pleased if you wake her up."

That and the fact she belongs here with me. "Yes. I'll bring her by early tomorrow. Would you still like to go to Piraeus?"

"Heck, yeah! I've been wanting to check out your yacht since you mentioned it!"

"The only reason why you've been nice to me, huh?"

"Part of it," Frankie deadpanned. "Be safe, kids."

"Have a good night, Frankie."

He hung up the phone and slid out of bed, kissing Samara's forehead quickly before going to his flat door and opening it. Spyros was on the other side, just about to knock.

He growled. "I hate it when you do that, cousin."

"I just got off the phone with Frankie."

"Did you?"

"Thank you for being a gentleman."

Spyros laughed. "As if she would let me be anything but!"

The cousins slapped each other's shoulders before going into their respective flats. AJ shut down his home and went back into bed, Samara still lying undisturbed from her slumber. He gathered her in his arms and joined her there.

The next morning AJ awoke alone. He sat up quickly, fear gripping his heart, dread following soon after, and finally foolishness bringing up the rear. His immediate thought was he'd been dreaming, but there was still a dip in the pillow beside him and there was a foreign, yet welcome sound from the foot of his bed. AJ crawled on the bed toward it, and smiled to see Samara on the floor. She was staring at their painting.

He moaned and kissed the top of her head. "Good morning, precious."

"Morning." Her voice was deep and husky, and it made his cock twitch. "Did I wake you?"

"Not at all." He hung off the side of the bed and kissed her cheek. Samara lifted her arms and hugged his neck as best she could.

"I'm an early riser."

"I know."

"You do?"

"Yes."

She laughed. "Okay, then."

"I guess I should take you to the hotel so you can change."

"Perhaps that would be best. Are we still going boating?"

"Yes. You should see the Greek Isles."

"Okay." She was about to stand, but AJ halted her process by placing gentle hands on her shoulders. She looked up at him curiously, but he merely grinned and kissed her nose, then her lips. Samara chuckled into his mouth, appreciating his upside-down buss.

"*Now* it is an excellent morning," he said, letting her stand. Samara scrunched up her nose in a most lovely fashion and went into the bathroom to change. As she did so, he went across the hall to Spyros's flat, telling a grumpy and rumpled Spyros to get ready so they could get to Piraeus before the tourist crowds overwhelmed.

"And why am I going again?" Spyros muttered, scratching his bare chest absently.

"Frankie."

Spyros woke up a little at that. "Ah, yes. Give me thirty."

Chuckling, AJ returned to his apartment, mildly surprised to see Samara already dressed. He went up to her and dragged his knuckles against her cheek. She blinked slowly and smiled softly at him.

"Did you sleep well?" he asked lowly.

"Yes. You?"

He nodded, tipping her face up to him and dragging his thumb along her lips. "Absolutely perfectly. I'm going to shower and get ready for our trip to Piraeus. Do you have a swimsuit?"

Her brows furrowed slightly. "Why?"

"Do you want to swim?"

A blush came into her cheeks. "I don't know about all that..."

AJ brushed his lips against her ear. "I can teach you if you don't know how."

"How kind of you," Samara said dryly.

He smiled and drew back. "Bring a swimsuit. Or we can skinny dip—"

"I don't think so," she said, arching an eyebrow.

He laughed and gave her a final kiss before letting her go. "Okay, sweet Samara. Bring the suit, though. I'm serious. We're getting you in that water."

Samara rolled her eyes. "May I use your phone?"

"You don't have to ask me to use anything, *khriso mou.*" *It's yours, sweet Samara. All yours.*

She gave him a smile and sat on the bed to undoubtedly call Frankie. AJ went into the bathroom and took a quick shower. When he came back out, Samara was still on the phone; but when she spotted him, her speech slurred to a stop.

"A-AJ!" she sputtered, though her eyes had a hard time meeting his.

He grinned roguishly at her. "Yes, my love?"

She glanced at him quickly, then averted her eyes, the blush strong on her cheeks. "I have to go, Frankie. I'll be there soon, okay?"

She put the phone on the base and kept her eyes away from him. She hurried out of his room and he let her, then allowed the towel that had been precarious hanging around his hips to finally fall. Samara had liked what she'd seen!

He put on his swim trunks, then khaki shorts and a white polo shirt, and slipped his feet in thongs. He grabbed a beach towel and sunscreen, then plucked his shades, keys, and mobile phone from his nightstand and met her in the living room. Spyros was there with her.

"All ready?" AJ asked, pressing a teasing kiss to Samara's cheek when he approached her. Spyros grinned at them and nodded.

"You're making her blush, cousin."

"I like it when she blushes," AJ said, winking at Spyros and laughing when Samara muttered something incomprehensible and started out of his flat first.

They made a quick stop to Melonakos where two baskets were awaiting them. Spyros had called down for lunch and dinner for four people and pastries for breakfast. Then they went to Samara's hotel, where AJ and Spyros waited in the lobby while the sisters got ready. When they finally came downstairs, both men went dry-mouthed and breathless. They were wearing similar summer dresses, Samara's was yellow while Frankie's was a pale blue. Frankie's dress was a halter while Samara's had straps that crisscrossed at the back. They had matching sandals on their feet and straw bags filled with items they might need during the day, including a light jacket.

AJ went to Samara and kissed her cheek. "You're stunning. Are you wearing a swimsuit?"

"You wanted me to put it on?"

"You have one?"

"Yes, AJ. I still don't think I'll need it, though."

"You will," AJ assured her, and linked their fingers together. "Come, let's go. The metro will be better than a taxi."

The ride to Piraeus was enjoyable, especially with Samara tucked into his side as he told her and Frankie about his favorite places to go while he sailed.

"We're avoiding the tourists' routes on this trip," he told them. "You have natives with you; we know the best places, anyway."

When they reached the marina, it was already packed. AJ held onto Samara's hand tightly as they weaved their way through the crowds toward the private vessels. His was moored between two boats of similar size, and a dockworker alighted from the boat.

"Hello, Ioannis," AJ said.

Ioannis nodded and spoke to them in Greek. He knew little English. "I did some light cleaning on the deck and made sure everything was working properly. She should be perfect."

"Thanks, Ioannis," AJ said, slipping him a generous tip. The dockworker inclined his head to the four of them before going off to the main building.

"This is *nice!*" Frankie exclaimed, stopping at the edge as if afraid to board. "Good job!"

AJ laughed and stepped onto his baby, the *Isis.* Spyros joined him, and the two helped the sisters board.

"This really is nice, AJ," Samara said, touching the rigging reverently. "And you know how to sail?"

"Yes," AJ said, giving them a tour of the deck, then below with the cabins.

"It has a stove, beds, and everything!" Frankie said excitedly. "The boat didn't look so big from the outside!"

"I told you it wasn't anything too elaborate," AJ said, laughing at Frankie's enthusiasm.

"It's wonderful," Samara determined, sitting down at the tiny table in the center of the galley.

"I'm glad you think so, my Samara," AJ rumbled.

Two sets of throats cleared as Samara blushed and looked around the cabin more.

"Come, Spyros," AJ said, "let's get *Isis* out to sea."

Frankie and Samara watched them unfurl the sails and do other chores as they got *Isis* out of the marina and into the Saronic Gulf. The weather was perfect—warm, but not too warm, and the breeze was present but gentle. The waters were calm as well, which allowed for little rocking of the boat. AJ kept the

Isis on a steady, unhurried pace, and the sisters spoke excitedly about all they saw.

AJ's eyes never strayed far from Samara. There was peace and joy on her face as she sat on the deck looking at the sea he loved so much. He could easily see them taking private tours together, snuggling together on the deck as they sipped wine. Making love above deck or below. It was the perfect honeymoon.

"Slow down, AJ," he whispered under his breath. "Slow down…"

Soon they were at a lagoon and he dropped anchor. Very few people knew about this place because it wasn't close to any historical sites, but AJ loved it for its clean, shallow waters, pristine beach, and purity from tourist traffic.

"Do you come here often?" Samara asked when he came to sit next to her. Spyros and Frankie were sitting close together as well, Spyros's arm around Frankie's shoulders.

"Right after I got the boat, Spyros, Dimitri, and Khristos, our American cousins, and I picked three random places on a map that we wanted to go. I chose Angistri. Most people go to the bigger island Aegina. This was mine. The other three fell in love with it, of course," AJ said with a grin.

Spyros rolled his eyes. "Rub it in…"

"But, yes, whenever we go boating, we generally come here. The tourist parts of the island are on the opposite side. Sometimes, there are other boats, but most of the time it's just us."

The four of them enjoyed the ocean breeze as they ate lunch, the boat rocking gently in the waves.

"Would you like to swim?" Spyros asked Frankie after they finished their meals. They had been sitting quietly, enjoying the sun and sway for a moment.

"Aren't we supposed to wait an hour or something like that?"

"Myth," AJ dismissed with a chuckle and brought a satiated Samara close to him. "We'll be fine. And we have life jackets just in case."

"So, how about it?"

Frankie eyed Spyros and touched her hair. "I can't get it wet!

"Why?"

Samara started snickering. AJ bent his mouth to her ear, delighting in her shiver. "Why can't she get it wet?"

"Her hair is relaxed."

"Relaxed?"

"Yes. Relaxed. It's straight, not...coiled like mine."

"Can you get yours wet?"

"My hair is natural, so yes, I can."

"So you have no excuse not to swim," he said, eyeing her.

"My pride and dignity would say otherwise."

"Why? Are you ashamed of your body, Samara?"

The way her eyes widened and the catch in her breath told him he'd guessed the crux of her dilemma. He skimmed his lips along her cheek and wrapped his arm across her belly. "Don't be, Samara. Your body is so lovely. So full, so womanly. I adore it as I adore you."

Samara leaned into his lips, and he kissed the corner of hers. "Come, precious. Let's swim."

"And if you can't swim, Frankie, we can always go to Aegina. Visit the sites there."

"I never said I was swimming—and I want to see sites too!" Samara insisted.

"Well, it'll be dull just watching you two swim while I sit here and don't do anything! You don't even have a deck of cards, do you?" she asked Spyros accusingly. He blushed and shook his head.

"The idea isn't bad, precious," AJ said. "And Spyros and I have mobile phones, so I'll dock and we can go see the sites also."

Samara and Frankie did that silent communication again before Samara nodded. "I can't believe I let you talk me into this."

"You love swimming, Samara," Frankie said, earning a smile from AJ and a glare from her sister. "And there're life jackets." She said the last part with a wink.

"I hate you."

"My love is like the ocean," Frankie said cheekily, blowing her sister a kiss.

"I'll take us to Aegina while you go downstairs and change, Samara," AJ said.

He docked at Skala where Spyros and Frankie could catch a ferry to Aegina, then took the boat around the island back to their more private space of water. He anchored the boat again, then went down below to check on Samara.

He noticed the shower door was closed and he knocked on it. "All right, Samara?"

"Yeah...just...give me a second."

He could hear her nervousness and he pressed a hand to the door. "Precious, if you are really that uncomfortable, you don't have to."

"I'll be fine," she assured him. "I just need a second to get my bearings. I'll be out soon. I'm sorry."

"You tell me when I'm being a cad, Samara," AJ said with a hint of a smile. "Sometimes I can be."

She laughed. "All right, AJ, I will."

Her laughter made him feel better. He went to one of the cabins and peeled out of his outerwear, and folded the clothes onto the bed. He then went back up on deck and made sure the life gear was secure.

"Okay," he heard Samara's apprehensive voice behind him. "I'm ready...I think."

He turned and saw her in a tank top and shorts. He looked at her oddly. "Samara?"

She didn't answer him, her eyes darting over his broad chest. He couldn't help but feel cocky at her pleased look, but he wouldn't be deterred.

"Precious."

"What?" Her eyes snapped to his and a blush stained those dark cheeks.

He smiled a little at her response to his endearment for her. "Where's your bathing suit?"

She huffed. "Underneath."

He went to her and toyed with the hem of the gray tank. "Then take these clothes off so we can swim."

SEVEN

"I can swim just fine in what I'm wearing," Samara said. "I promised I would go swimming, and I am."

AJ fit his hands on her waist and he grinned at her shiver. His eyes completely focused on hers, he slid his hands up her body, over the curves of her breasts, to her shoulders. He squeezed them softly.

"Okay, little Samara. You win. Like I said, I want you to be comfortable. Will you allow me to be comfortable too?"

Her eyes became wary, but she nodded anyway. AJ grinned broader, and he stepped away. His eyes remained focused on her as he shucked off his swimming trunks. Her eyes widened, skipped down his body, and then jerked back up to his eyes. She then spun around and started back down below.

Chuckling, AJ wrapped his arm around her waist and brought her body against his, his length hardening in reaction to feeling her.

"Samara," he cooed into her ear, his other arm coming around her, effectively trapping her in his embrace.

She wiggled, then moaned as she felt him against her bum. "You're naked, AJ!"

"Yes. You said I could get comfortable."

"Are you a nudist?"

"Not usually," AJ said, nipping the curve of her ear, "but I have a confession. Ever since meeting you, I've had a never-ending erection, and the sight of you right now was too much...so I had to, you see. Otherwise, I'd be in too much pain to swim!"

"Swim."

AJ nipped at her ear again, his hand sliding underneath her tank to feel the fabric of her swimsuit. He moved his hand lower and felt another hem, then the elastic of her shorts.

"A two-piece, Samara?"

"Don't sound so smug," she snapped, her body trembling even more when his hand touched her bare stomach.

"AJ, please let go of me."

There was fear in her tone, and AJ immediately complied. She still didn't turn to meet him, and that made him hurt a little. "I thought you trusted me, Samara."

"I do."

"Then why won't you look at me? Swim? I'm not forcing you to do anything, and I never will. I just want you to relax. Let go. You can be yourself with me, Samara. That's all I ask of you. To be yourself, completely and only yourself. I won't hurt you. I'd die before I hurt you, Samara. I wish you'd believe that of me."

With that, AJ jumped off the side of the boat and into the cool water. He needed to calm down and get himself back in order. Despite the many caddish tendencies he had, his mother had raised him to be a gentleman, and Samara deserved nothing less. He had to remember she was inexperienced, and anything too insistent could make her skittish and closed off. He wanted her to relax, to enjoy their time. Perhaps he'd pushed things too far by shucking off his clothes, but if that were the only way he could be as vulnerable as she seemed to be, even while fully clothed, then so be it.

"Do you know how deep the water is?"

AJ spun around to see Samara hanging onto the swim ladder on the boat, completely submerged in the water.

"Not too deep," he assured her, smiling at the appealing picture she made. "But don't worry. I won't let you sink."

She gave him a tiny scowl, gripping the ladder tighter. She took a deep breath. "Okay...you can do this, Sam..."

He began swimming to her. "Do you need any help? I meant what I said, I can teach you if you need to learn how to swim."

"I was taught," Samara said absently, though she seemed to shrink against the boat the closer he came to her. He stopped a little away from her and began treading water. He looked at her carefully, and when he finally realized what was up, another part of his anatomy was up and pulsating as well.

She was nude.

There were no straps on her shoulders, and he knew for a fact the swimsuit she'd been wearing had straps. Also, given the way her cheeks were redder than normal, it seemed she realized he figured out what her current state was.

"Samara?" he asked, confused and a little humbled. "Why?"

She shrugged and took a deep breath, licking her lips. "You asked me to trust you. I said I did, but…I haven't been proving that very well. You also said you wouldn't hurt me, and I do believe that too. So…I'm doing the final thing you wanted me to do—being myself. This is she, every inch of her. I don't think I'm ever going to get smaller, but I will probably get larger, so if you can't handle that—"

His mouth cut off the rest of the rambling coming from hers, he finally crossing the final distance between them to do so. He gathered her body to him, felt it tremble so violently that he broke the kiss and tucked her face into his neck.

"*Shh*, my love," he murmured into her wet hair. He caressed her bare back gently. "It's okay. Relax. Just feel me. Get used to my body."

She was so soft and pliant. He loved the armful she made, how every one of her curves fit into his hard body. He swam them over to the ladder and set her on a rung, but still kept her close. Her breasts mashed into his chest, her nipples hard. Soft, womanly. How could she think he wouldn't find her glorious?

"I love how you feel in my arms, Samara," he continued to whisper, stroking her back. "You fit me, love. You fit me perfectly. God made you for me. Don't you see? Can't you feel it?"

He took one of her hands and put it on his chest, right above his heartbeat. "Touch me, Samara. Explore me. Just like you did in the gardens. I'm yours. Completely yours."

He dropped his arms from around her and held onto the ladder instead, standing on the lowest rung on the ladder so his upper body was out of the water and that her hands had better access. Her eyes skipped to his briefly before they fell upon his neck. Her hands followed, damp, cool, and fleeting as they danced upon his skin. Though it was summer, it felt like he was being touched by snowflakes, so light was her caress. AJ tilted his head back so she had even more access to skin, and he purred low in his throat when her hand completely went around his neck.

Those hands moved lower, firmer this time, leaving no part of his chest untouched. He had a modest sprinkling of hair, but she didn't seem to mind. Her fingers worried his nipples. They tightened, but AJ kept his head tilted back and toward the sky, allowing her complete privacy.

She moved lower still, over his abdomen, tickling his navel. His stomach dipped and he chuckled a little.

"Are you ticklish, AJ?"

He looked down at her face, making sure not to look anywhere else. "Not as ticklish as you are."

Her smile widened. "I'm a good girl. I won't tickle you."

"No. You'll just make me horny instead!"

"AJ!"

"Samara!" he mimicked on a laugh. "You think I'm a monk? You, touching me? I'm as hard as stone right now!"

Her eyes glanced down. The water couldn't hide his state, and she turned beet red.

"Have you ever seen a man like this before, Samara?" he asked, all trace of humor gone.

"Porn doesn't count, does it?"

He twitched. He couldn't help it. He heard her gasp and saw her blush even more. "You watch porn?"

"Women get horny too," Samara said with a defensive edge.

"Does it turn you on?"

She shrugged and dropped her head. "Sometimes."

Passion. He grinned, but dropped that particular subject for now. "But you've never seen one in real life. A real, hard penis?"

"No."

"Which means you've never touched one."

"No, it doesn't."

He twitched again, but this time in jealousy. "Care to explain?"

She arched an eyebrow at him. "You can touch something without seeing it. A boy shoves your hand down his pants, you feel things, AJ," Samara said sarcastically.

"And how did it feel?"

She grimaced. "Slimy. Weird. I didn't like it."

"Would you like to try again? This time with sight and all?"

Before she could pull her hand away, AJ pressed it against his lower abdomen, right above the black thatch of hair on his pelvis. Her fingers flexed underneath his, and he groaned, resting his forehead against hers.

"I'd like you to touch me. To feel what you do to me. I've never been so hard in my life, Samara," he whispered. "Please. Touch me."

He felt her hand begin to tremble underneath his, but she let out a soft breath. "Okay."

He nodded, his forehead still against hers, then pulled back to kiss it as he removed his hand from hers and gripped the ladder again. His hardness kept twitching in anticipation, he couldn't help it, and he prayed to God he would be able to keep it together once her hand closed around him.

He barely held on. Her hand was smooth, warm, and wet, and he jerked so violently that startled eyes met his.

"Did I hurt you?"

"No, baby," AJ groaned. "Just give me a minute...your hot little hand. Damn, Samara..."

She slid up her hand, her thumb going over the tip of him. He jerked again, and he cupped her cheek, drifting his mouth over her forehead and nose.

"This all right?" she asked as his lips found hers.

"Perfect," AJ murmured, shuddering at the sensations he was feeling. "Move your hand, precious. Stroke me. Feel me."

She did, and AJ pumped into her ministrations. Their mouths never drifted far from each other, but they didn't kiss. Instead, they shared breath, nibbling at lips, licking the salt and unique flavor of each other. Never before had his climax rushed so fast, like a tornado that appeared from nowhere, and he enclosed his hand around hers.

"Stop before I come," he whispered, and he gave her a proper kiss.

"What if I want you to?"

That was absolutely the wrong thing for her to say. The devil awakened in him and he put his mouth to her ear. "*Khriso mou*, the only place I want to come is inside that hot little body of yours. I want to feel you clench around me and milk me for all I'm worth. I want to fill you with my seed, to know I'm the first, and will damn well be the last to know the paradise that lies between your thighs."

She sighed and shuddered, squeezing his cock so that he had no choice but to come. He collapsed against her, his lips buried into her neck as he wrapped his shaky arms around her. She snuggled into him, sighing again.

"So much for being inside you," AJ muttered against her skin. He smiled at her answering tremor.

"If it makes you feel any better, I came too."

It did. "Only from my words, Samara? I can make you shudder and shatter with only my words? My voice?"

He licked her skin, and she shuddered again. She had so much passion, and he couldn't wait to make it bloom.

AJ began kissing lower, along her collarbone, and her shivers picked up more. He was only grazing his lips on her skin, and still she reacted. She felt everything so keenly. He loved it.

Samara was breathing deeply, and the way her nipples brushed his chest with each breath made him moan against her skin. AJ sank lower in the water, his mouth following suit along her body. Her breasts were magnificent, and he nuzzled his face in her bosom, delighting in her nipples grazing his nose and cheeks.

"AJ," she whispered, arching her back slightly so her breasts would touch more of him.

So she was sensitive? This fact pleased him.

"Yes, precious?" he asked, bringing his mouth ever closer to one nipple. He exhaled, and she shook.

Moaned.

Wanting to hear that again, but louder, he darted his tongue out and lifted her nipple with it. Her hand immediately sank into his hair and he smiled, his lips brushing against her distended peak.

"Do you touch yourself, Samara?" he asked, making sure his lips touched her as he spoke.

She didn't answer right away, but then, "Yes."

"Play with your other nipple for me," he ordered, his green eyes dark with lust as they looked at her. Her eyes remained on his, and she slowly slid her hand down her chest until she cupped a heavy breast in her hand. AJ watched her thumb circle the dark-brown peak, fascinated by how quickly, with just the lightest of touches, it immediately tightened. He focused on the breast he had and used two hands to hold it. He studied it, every ridge of the areola, how swollen the actual tip was. Her breasts were as exquisite as he had imagined they would be when he'd first seen her.

"These are things of beauty," AJ murmured right before suckling on the enticing tip. Samara's gasp was symphonic. His fingers caressed the underside of her breast as he sucked, and her hand that wasn't on her other breast slid into his hair. Her hips began to buck slightly, and AJ groaned in approval. Damn it all, but she was so sexy.

He pressed her nipple onto the roof of his mouth and used his tongue to stroke it, adding to the sensations she would feel. Her body trembled and the fingers in his hair clutched him. Her whimper made his length swell and harden more.

"AJ," she moaned. When had her voice become so deep and passion-filled?

AJ let go of her nipple and moved his mouth to the southern curve of her breast. Her nipple grazing the bridge of his nose was almost his undoing, but he licked at the seam of her breast, delighted in her trembles and gasps. He took her free hand and drew it lower even as he encouraged her to sit on a higher ladder rung.

Reluctantly, he pulled back to give her more room; and soon, her entire body was out of the water, visible to his heady gaze.

Soft. She was all soft, dark gold. She was wholly a woman. Unable to help himself, he buried his face into her marshmallow stomach, earning the most charming giggle from her, and he smiled against her skin. His hands met at the small of her back and he pressed kiss upon kiss on her belly. Unbidden came the image of her swollen with his legacy, and he placed a reverent buss above her womb. This was to be the future resting place of whatever children he was supposed to have. This was the womb in which they would grow, the body from which they would be born. The realization humbled and thrilled him.

His mouth traveled lower, and he noticed her giggles gave way to gasps and tiny whimpers. He smiled once more, pulling back slightly to look into her deep-brown eyes.

"Samara," he said softly with a tiny grin.

"AJ," she returned. She couldn't hide her tremors, and he stroked the small of her back to relax her.

He took one of her hands in his and placed it between her legs, keeping his eyes locked with hers.

"AJ?"

"Show me how you bring yourself pleasure, my love," he murmured softly. He needed tips. It wasn't the same for every woman.

"What?"

"Stroke yourself. Caress yourself for me. I want to know how you bring yourself to climax, so that I may know how to do the same when it's my turn."

"Damn, AJ..."

He pressed her hand against her mound. It was unshaven and wet from the water and her own essence. Her nub was pink, swollen, and larger than what he'd seen on most of the women he had known. It would be perfect to suck.

But not now. Later.

He lifted her index finger and traced it around her knot. She bucked her hips.

"Show me," he whispered against the inside of her thigh.

Her hand shook as she slowly slipped her middle finger into the moist opening below. He growled against her thigh, wishing it were a certain part of his anatomy entering that wonderful sheath, and groaned when she pulled her finger out, coated with her juices. That finger circled the bundle of nerves above her entrance, and it seemed to harden and swell even more. She used firm strokes to bring herself to climax. AJ was fascinated by her and her ritual. She seemed to prefer external stimulation; but given how tight she had been when he'd touched her that first time, AJ could understand.

"Shit!"

AJ grinned at her expletive. He'd slipped two fingers inside her, and her fingers had stopped as her inner muscles clenched him so tightly. He nipped at her sensitive skin close to her nether lips.

"Are you okay, Samara?" he asked softly.

"Mmm, *yes...*"

He smiled and kissed her inner thigh. "Enjoy."

He stroked her slowly, making sure she felt every thrust of his fingers. Hers hovered above her entrance, unsure and inviting. With a groan, he slipped her fingers into his mouth to taste her, and her answering whimper had him bucking against the swim ladder in an automatic reaction.

"You taste like you look, *khriso mou,*" AJ said lowly, smacking his lips obscenely. "Delicious. I need more."

He moved too quickly for her to protest, and soon he gave her a broad lick from where his fingers were up to her swollen flesh. Samara jerked and moaned, and he used his free hand to stroke her tummy to calm her.

"Has anyone ever tasted you before, Samara?" he asked, his lips brushing against her searing, plump center.

"N-no..."

"May I taste you again, sweet Samara?" He chuckled then and kissed her nub again. "Definitely sweet. With a little tang."

It seemed she'd grown slicker as he spoke, and there were audible squishy sounds as he pumped his fingers in and out of her. How he wanted to replace them with his cock, but he hadn't brought any protection. Though he wanted to leave her with something to remember him by, he didn't think his child was a souvenir she'd like.

Besides, he would give her his last name before he gave her the babies to go along with it.

Nevertheless, AJ put his tongue on her again, relishing in her moans. The sensation of her pubic hair only heightened his own ardor, and he made sure no part of her core was left untouched by his tongue and lips. Her body quaked fiercely, and her fingers tangled into his hair almost painfully. She was trying to say his name, but all she could get out was "A..."

He loved making her speechless.

AJ gripped her bum and brought her core to his mouth. He looked along her body, groaned at the way her breasts thrust up to the heavens, and thanked God He allowed such a woman to be with him.

"Let me taste you, sweet Samara," he muttered against her, surging his tongue inside her. He knew she was close. "Let me taste your ecstasy."

Samara did, and she wasn't stingy with her offering. AJ took every single drop of her pleasure onto his tongue. Her fingers eventually released the death grip they had on his hair. He moved up her body, kissing, nipping, and suckling all the way. He paid homage to her breasts again, causing husky laughter to leave her mouth, and he laughed against her skin. She wrapped her arms around his neck and purred when his lips pressed tiny kisses upon the column of her throat. Finally, he became level with her face, and he cupped her cheek tenderly.

"Would you like to taste something sweet, Samara?" he asked cheekily.

She bit her lip, blushed hard, but nodded. Good girl.

At first, he pecked her lips, creating a sound of protest from her. AJ smiled and kissed her harder, still closed-mouthed, but he wrapped his arms around her waist and brought her flush against him in a slow manner. To his joy and consternation, Samara wrapped her arms around his neck and her legs around his hips, bringing her hot core in direct contact with his hardness. AJ groaned into her mouth, opening it to slide his tongue inside to tangle with hers. She'd gotten considerably more comfortable with kissing since the first time they'd done so, and his body was ready and willing to introduce her to another level of lovemaking. But he had to be responsible.

With a great deal of regret and longing, AJ broke the kiss and touched his forehead to hers. Her fingers caressed the nape of his neck, and she wore the most contented smile on her face.

"We should go to Aegina," AJ murmured against her mouth.

She grinned and drifted her nose along his. "We didn't do much swimming, babe."

"Disappointed?"

"That this has to end? Yes."

AJ pulled back and grasped her chin, shaking his head. "Not end. It's just on hold. This *will* be continued at another time."

Her eyes grew sad. AJ, not pleased with that reaction, nodded and shook her chin gently. "I mean it, Samara. We just started. This isn't over."

Instead of answering, Samara hugged him. They held each other for a long while before they climbed back on the boat deck. They showered separately, AJ relieved the stall was too small to share it, and redressed in their street clothes. He stood behind her as he helped her steer the boat to the dock. Once the boat was moored, AJ called Spyros and told them they were on the island. Spyros suggested they meet back at the marina whenever he and Samara were done; Frankie and Spyros would be on the boat by then. AJ agreed to the plan and took Samara to the highlights of the small island. The main one was the Temple of Aphaia; and once again, Samara's love for Greek mythology took over.

"I've never heard of her," Samara said, as if a bit ashamed of her ignorance. When they learned she was the local deity of fertility and agriculture, AJ couldn't help but smirk and steal a glimpse at Samara's direction. She felt his eyes on her and glanced at him, and blushed when she saw that look in his eyes.

"So bad," she muttered.

"That wasn't what you were saying an hour ago, love," AJ murmured back.

Her gasp had him biting back a chuckle, and he lifted their joined hands to kiss the back of hers. For the next hour or so they toured the temple. Samara wished she had a camera with her; but knowing Frankie, her sister would have covered her on that front.

AJ frowned. "Why don't you have a camera?"

Samara shrugged. "I end up forgetting them, so I don't bother."

He wrapped his arms around her shoulders and kissed her forehead. "We'll always have our painting."

She snuggled into him. "Definitely won't forget that."

They left the temple soon afterward and Samara begged off buying any souvenirs in favor of going back to the boat. Her voice was solemn as she said they needed to return to Athens so she and Frankie could get ready for their flight tomorrow morning.

Damn. That pesky little matter.

Neither spoke on the way back to the marina. When they reached the *Isis*, Frankie and Spyros were already eating the dinner Melonakos had prepared for them. The sisters gave warm smiles to each other; and with a tiny squeeze to AJ's hand, Samara walked off to chat and eat with Frankie. AJ's moves were mechanical as he unmoored the boat.

"Are you all right, cousin?" Spyros asked as he began to help.

"Would you be all right if the woman you loved was leaving for an indefinite amount of time in a few hours?"

Spyros squeezed AJ's shoulder and assisted AJ with the rest of the chores. As they were on the water heading back to the Piraeus port, Spyros told AJ to eat and that he could navigate. Knowing his cousin made sense, AJ went to the deck where Samara and Frankie were still eating, well, more Samara than Frankie. He sat next to Samara and wrapped an arm around her waist.

"Was the food all right, ladies?" AJ asked, using one hand to grab his own meal of lamb wraps.

The sisters nodded. "I'm going to miss it when we leave tomorrow," Frankie said. "I think we need a recipe or something."

"Only works while in Greece. Something about the sun," AJ said teasingly.

Samara leaned into him and smiled at her sister. "Maybe they make international deliveries?"

"I'll definitely look into the prospect for you, my love," AJ murmured, kissing her temple and squeezing her ever closer.

If Frankie had heard the endearment, she pretended she didn't, and started talking about how many things she had to pack for the flight. Again, AJ and Samara spoke little; and when Frankie realized she was holding a conversation with herself, she stopped talking and enjoyed the sun setting over the ocean.

"Beautiful," Samara murmured on behalf of the group. Spyros had returned briefly to share in the sight, his hands gentle on Frankie's shoulders.

AJ nuzzled Samara's cheek but said nothing, all the while thinking whom he held in his arms was infinitely more beautiful.

EIGHT

The metro went too quickly for AJ's liking. Sooner than he preferred, they were in front of the Marina Hotel once more. The group went into the lobby and said their goodbyes.

"What time is your flight tomorrow?" AJ asked, his fingers still intertwined with Samara's.

"It's really early. Seven in the morning," Samara said apologetically. "We have to leave here around four-thirty to be on time."

"Samara..." He framed her face in his hands and closed his eyes. How could he let her leave? His heart felt as if concrete had been poured over it, making it impossible to beat.

"Perhaps we should exchange contact information now, huh?" she whispered. He could hear a sob beginning to form.

"I don't want you to go," AJ returned just as softly.

Samara took a deep breath, and then buried her face in his chest. AJ held her fast to him, his face concealed by the top of her head. He loved her. He loved this woman. Somewhere deep inside him, he knew she loved him in return. It wasn't right they had to be separated like this.

"I'll be here in the morning," he vowed. "Don't worry about the taxi; I'll get it for you. Four-thirty."

"Thank you," Samara said. "But you don't have to—"

"I do," AJ murmured. "You know I do. We'll exchange information then."

She nodded and pulled back, sliding trembling fingers along his cheeks. They then went across his lips and his nose, and his eyelids fluttered shut.

"Wow, I'm going to miss you."

"Not for long," AJ said, lifting up his mouth to kiss her palm. "We won't be separated for long."

AJ bent his head and kissed her softly before she could respond. "Sweet dreams, Samara. See you in a few hours."

Both he and Spyros were solemn and quiet on their way to their flat building.

"Are you coming with me tomorrow morning?" AJ asked when they reached their individual doors.

"Yeah," Spyros said. "I'd like to say goodbye."

AJ nodded once. "Then I suggest we'd get some sleep."

As soon as he entered his flat, he placed a call to a local taxi service and requested a pick up at four in the morning in front of the flat building. Afterward, he undressed and climbed into bed, but he was too wired to sleep. His mind kept thinking of the life he had begun to plan with Samara since seeing her in the market. Five days? Five days might as well be five minutes as far as AJ was concerned. It wasn't long enough, yet he shouldn't be ungrateful for God's gift. That was what Samara was, a gift. His and his alone. How could he in good conscience let her get on that plane to fly out of his life for who knew how long? He would, though, because it was to be.

For now.

"It's not over," he whispered to his dark ceiling. He thought he could still smell her, could still feel her warmth as she'd curled up next to him in slumber the night before. She'd snuggled into him as if they'd been doing it all their lives. And if AJ had anything to say about it, they would.

He fell into a catnap, but he'd set the alarm on his clock to wake him at three. It rang too soon for his liking, and not only because he'd gotten minimal rest. He was in no hurry for Samara to leave his life, no matter how temporary the absence would be. Thirty-four years without her had been long enough.

AJ shuffled around, his movements lethargic as he took a shower and slipped on a nondescript shirt and trousers. He made sure he had his identification and keys before going across the hall and knocking on Spyros's door.

AJ was mildly surprised to see his cousin fully dressed.

"Alarm," Spyros said roughly. His curly hair was messy atop his head, but neither man really cared. It was too early in the morning to impress anyone.

"Let's go," AJ said. Spyros clapped his shoulder and AJ smiled a little, grateful for his cousin's support.

The taxi came a few minutes after four, but it wouldn't take long to get to the Marina since there was no traffic this early. When they reached the hotel, AJ asked the driver to wait. Both he and Spyros went into the lobby to greet the sisters. They came down twenty minutes after the hour. Both girls packed incredibly light—only one small roller suitcase and a carry-on for each. Nevertheless, both men took their luggage and assisted them in getting into the taxi.

The ride to the airport was quiet. AJ looked behind him to see Frankie and Spyros curled into each other in slumber. Samara wasn't sleeping, but her eyes were soft and a little sad as she met his gaze. They stared at each other until the taxi arrived at the airport.

"Terminal?" the driver asked in Greek, and AJ translated for Samara.

"Alitalia," Samara murmured, all the while looking at AJ. AJ repeated it in Greek, still staring at Samara. As soon as the taxi pulled in front of the terminal, Samara dropped her eyes and got out the car. The lack of movement awakened the other two backseat passengers, but they didn't rush to disembark. Once again, Spyros and AJ gathered the sisters' luggage, and the four made their way to the counter. The lines were already long, which amazed AJ, but he wasn't upset. It increased the time they had together.

Samara leaned against his hard body, her eyes closed, as they stood in line. AJ wrapped an arm around her waist and kept her close. They only moved when necessary. They didn't speak. What could they say? Too many things, and nothing that would keep her here in Greece.

Frankie and Spyros were talking in low tones ahead of them. Spyros had his address book out and Frankie was filling in the information. He and Samara would have to do the same.

Eventually.

Twenty minutes later, Samara and Frankie were being checked in, he and Spyros standing off to the side. Samara's smile was kind as she interacted with the attendant, but not nearly as bright as he'd seen before. The sisters checked their luggage and received their boarding passes, then moved away from the counter toward them.

"Well," Samara said, trying desperately to keep her tone light, but he could hear the sob just beneath the surface. "Guess this is it." They had to go soon. The line for security check was almost as long as the one to get their boarding passes.

"We need to exchange information, Samara," AJ reminded her.

"Oh! Yeah...yeah."

"Let's go in the security check line while y'all do that," Frankie suggested, her eyes understanding as she gazed upon them.

"This is why you're the smart sister," Samara teased. Frankie scoffed but smiled.

Frankie and Spyros stood ahead of them again. Spyros lent AJ the address book. He didn't trust himself to put such precious information on a loose piece of paper. Samara pulled a worn notebook from her carry-on, and they traded books and wrote down all of their contact information. When they were done, AJ returned the address book to Spyros and she put her notebook back in her carry-on. Then, AJ pulled her into a hug.

"I forgot the wine," AJ murmured.

"That's all right," she said, and squeezed his waist with her arms.

"It's not too late to stay," AJ said. He had to try, at least.

"I gotta go."

"You don't want to."

It was a statement, not a question, and her shaking head confirmed it.

"We'll talk every day."

She laughed sardonically, and he frowned. "Reminds me of all those summer camps I used to go to. People would make that promise to each other and then two months later everyone went back to being the strangers they'd been earlier that year."

"That won't happen with us," AJ said. "The soul never forgets its mate."

Her hands clutched his shirt at his sides. "This isn't fair."

"No, it isn't."

"Why couldn't you be American?"

"Why couldn't you be Greek?"

"You'd rather I be white?"

"I'd *rather*," AJ began, his eyes narrowing, "you were just as you are, but from Greece. That way you wouldn't be boarding this plane right now." Their difference in color hadn't come up during their entire time together, so why was she trying to bring it up now?

"Even if I were Greek I wouldn't have to be from Athens."

"And if I were American, I wouldn't have to be from Philadelphia."

Her shoulders fell and she hugged him tighter. "Unfair."

They were getting close to the checkpoint. They clung to each other. AJ knew intellectually he would have to drop his arms from around her, but his heart...that stubborn muscle... ruled his body right then.

"Samara?"

Frankie's voice broke through. Only four people were ahead of them from the checkpoint. The final moments had arrived.

AJ pulled back and framed her face. Tears stood in her eyes as she met his gaze. He murmured for her not to cry in Greek, bending his head to kiss those deep-brown eyes of hers. The tears slipped out, and he kissed them away as well. Finally, his lips hovered above hers.

"I lo—"

"Kiss me goodbye, AJ," Samara demanded. "Just kiss me goodbye and let me go."

AJ did as told, giving her the lightest, sweetest kiss he'd ever given a woman. She stood on her tiptoes to get everything out of the kiss he was giving her, her arms deliciously constricting around his waist.

"Samara..."

She let out a sob at the sound of her name and broke the kiss. She went flatfooted and hurried into the checkpoint, crossing into a place where he couldn't follow.

But his heart did.

He and Spyros stood and watched the sisters go deeper into the terminal. Not once did they look back. AJ ran a rough hand over his face and spun around, feeling his entire body starting to shatter from the loss. Spyros squeezed his shoulder but said nothing. There were no words that could comfort him.

Spyros took over for him, signaling for the taxi, telling the driver where they needed to go. He even convinced AJ to go to his flat and he'd cover his shift the restaurant. AJ was grateful for Spyros's concern and initiative. He wouldn't be much use today.

AJ fell asleep. Only he hadn't known he'd fallen asleep until he heard his mobile phone ring. He looked at the clock. It was a little after two in the afternoon, Spyros checking on him.

"I'm fine," he muttered, then hung up his phone and went back to sleep.

The phone woke him up again who knew how much later, and he cursed before fumbling on the nightstand to find his mobile.

"What?" he growled into the phone.

"AJ?"

He sat up quickly, not expecting the voice on the other end, at least not so soon. "Samara?"

She gave a nervous laugh and he wished he was there to nuzzle away her nerves. "Hi, um...I know it's late there but..."

He checked his alarm. It was after nine in the evening his time. "You can call me any time, Samara. Any time at all."

"I just wanted to call and say we made it to the States safely."

"Thank you for telling me. I'm glad to hear that."

"Thank you for everything, AJ."

"You're welcome," he said, "It was my joy to meet you."

Samara sighed and her voice dropped. "I feel empty, AJ. Lost. Listless. I feel cold."

"I feel all those things, too, Samara," AJ said, his tone matching hers. "But above all, I feel lo—"

"I miss you, AJ," Samara interrupted. "Thank you for the best five days of my life."

It was the second time she'd cut him off from expressing his feelings. "Why won't you let me say it?"

"Say what?"

"What I feel for you. How much I feel for you. How deeply and forever I feel for you."

Samara was quiet for a long moment. Oh, how he wished he could see her face, those deep-brown eyes again. AJ crawled out of bed and sat on the floor at the foot of it, staring at the painting that was still leaning against the wall beside his dresser. At first sight. At first touch. His body had known who she was before his brain had. His soul had homed onto her before the rest of him could catch up. Now she was an ocean away.

"Damn!"

"Are you all right?"

"No," AJ said, sliding a hand through his hair. "You need to be here with me, Samara. Beside me. I need to hold you every night and kiss you every morning. I need to give you my last name and my children. I need to lo—"

"But you *can't*!" Samara sobbed, cutting him off once more. "I can't...you can't *say those things to me* while you're over there and I'm over here! I can't! I can't...oh, AJ, I *miss you so much*! I need...oh, God!"

His arms ached to hold her; his lips burned to kiss away her tears. AJ now understood why she wouldn't let him say what he wanted to say. It would make it real. It would make it impossible to ignore. Perhaps this was why he was still able to function, even if barely. Had Samara told him she loved him, there was no way he would've ever let her get on that plane.

"So...this is what you want?" AJ asked softly.

"No," she said just as quietly. "But I never thought I'd ever be in a position to have what I do want. I wasn't ready or prepared for you, AJ. I need to get ready for you."

"You *are* ready, love. All I ever want or need is you."

"Mentally," Samara continued and chuckled. "Even spiritually. There are a lot of things I have to consider."

"What about your heart, Samara?" AJ asked. "Will you consider that?"

She was quiet for a few seconds. "I *miss you*, AJ. So much. I just wanted to call and tell you thank you for the week and that we got home safely."

"You're not home, Samara," AJ said firmly. "That's just the place where you live. But your home? That's with me. And you know it."

"In Greece?" she asked, her voice a little harder.

"With me. We can be in bloody Antarctica, but that would be home. You, me, together."

"Goodnight, AJ," Samara whispered, then ended the call.

Irritated, AJ tossed the phone aimlessly behind him before dropping his forehead to his raised knees. He didn't cry, no matter how intensely his eyes stung. Samara was terrified, and that terror seemed to outweigh whatever feelings she had for him. Though AJ was upset, he also understood Samara's need to situate herself. She seemed to find comfort in routine, and what had happened between them had been anything but. Samara also had a strong sense of responsibility, and for her to just drop everything in Philadelphia to be with him would go against everything she was, everything he had fallen in love with inside of her. He would have to be patient, even if he weren't the world's most patient man. For Samara, however, he would wait. He had no choice. She held his heart, after all.

Despite the late hour, AJ took a shower and changed before going to Melonakos. It was still packed, but the wait staff and patrons gave him sympathetic glances as he weaved his way through the dining area.

As soon as he saw Spyros notice him, the younger man's eyes widened and he made a beeline for the back. AJ quickly caught up with him.

"Gossip!" AJ growled in Greek as soon as he grabbed the back of Spyros's shirt.

"*Hijo.*"

That stopped both of them.

"Auntie—"

"Don't you have patrons to tend to, *sobrino*?"

Spyros yanked his shirt out of AJ's grasp and scurried back into the dining area, his sigh of relief audible and almost comical had AJ been in a lighter mood.

"Mama—"

"*Cállate, Alejandro. Necesito hablar contigo, por favor.*"

It wasn't a request, and AJ knew it. "Sí, Mama. *¿En la oficina?*"

"*Bueno. Después de ti.*"

AJ led them into the small office full of pictures from the Greek Isles and Athens. His mother, of whom AJ was the spitting image, sat down regally behind the desk in the top-of-the-line office chair AJ had purchased for himself, leaving AJ to occupy the straight-back wooden chair in front of it.

"Mama—"

"Alejandro, *mi amor, por favor*," his mother pleaded, her eyes full of concern and a little chastisement. "*Espera.*"

Luz Melonakos regarded her son carefully, as if trying to weigh her words. It was hard for him not to squirm. She used to look at him like this when he was younger, right before giving him a most awful punishment for misbehaving.

"*¿Quien es la mujer?*"

"*¿Con permiso?*" There was no reason for the question to catch him off guard. Of course his mother would want to know about the woman who'd occupied her son's time for the past week!

Luz rolled her eyes. "*¡Ay, Alejandro! ¡Oiste lo que dije!*"

AJ blushed. "*Sí, Mama.*"

"*¿Así?*"

AJ looked at his hands before responding. "*Se llama Samara y ella es de los Estados Unidos,* Philadelphia. *Ella tiene veinticuatro años y es muy bella. La amo.*"

"*¿Y por qué no conocí a ella?*"

"*No pensaba. Lo siento.*"

He'd been too preoccupied to worry about introductions, too concerned with spending as much time with Samara as possible for him to let her meet anyone else. Then again, had Samara *stayed...*

"*¿Y por qué ella no está aquí? ¿Ella no te ama? ¿La conociste por mucho tiempo?*"

"*Una semana. Realmente, cinco dias.*"

Luz nodded, then a slow grin formed on her face. "Love at first sight?" she asked in Greek.

"Yes," AJ said, returning her smile. "Love at first sight. Mama, she's lovely. So sweet. Shy, vulnerable. Wonderful. And she's very smart."

"She's your match," Luz said, her eyes showing her amusement.

He smiled fondly. "Yes, she is."

"And she went back to America?"

AJ nodded. "This morning. I feel like there's a gaping hole inside me, Mama."

Luz's eyes grew sad and they drifted to a framed photo of herself and her late husband, AJ's father. Kyriakos Melonakos had been dead for five years. His parents had married young; and by the time his father had passed on, they had experienced thirty years of wedded bliss.

AJ reached across the desk and held his mother's hand. He didn't know what to say to comfort her. Here he was, mourning over a woman who, while not here, was at least still alive. The love of his mother's life was not. He felt like an inconsiderate cad.

"I'm sorry."

"No, *mijo*," Luz said, squeezing her son's hand. "It's okay." She had switched to English. "Tell me more about your woman and when I will get to meet her. I have to say, I've never seen you smile so much than during the past week...when I saw you, that is."

AJ grinned and kissed the palm of his mother's hand. "*Te amo*, Mama."

"*Y tú, hijo, y tú.*"

It was close to midnight when he was finally ready to go home. He offered to close up since Spyros had covered for him throughout the day. His mother lived above the restaurant with Spyros's parents, so he walked her upstairs and said goodnight to them all before coming back down to shut down. He'd closed out the cash register when his eyes drifted to the table where Samara and Frankie had eaten their first night here. He didn't even know why she had been in Greece, and really didn't care. All he knew was she belonged in his restaurant, his home, his life. He went to the table and sat down before using his mobile to dial her number.

"Hello?" she answered after the third ring.

"I miss you, Samara," AJ said quietly. "Come home."

Samara took in a deep breath. "We probably need this separation right now, AJ. Slow things down."

"For what?" AJ asked. "This separation won't change anything. We belong together. You know it, and I know it."

"We don't really know each other," Samara said, ever practical. At the moment, AJ wished she could be reckless and get on another plane back to him.

Then again...

"Okay, then. We get to know each other. When's your birthday?"

Samara chuckled. "June 7th."

"Mine is February 4th," AJ said, a slow smile spreading across his face. "I think you're adorable."

"I think so too," Samara said jokingly.

"Yes," he said, his smile fading. "I adore you, Samara."

Her giggles petered out. "I like being adored by you," she admitted on a whisper.

"Then come back to me. Come home so I can adore you properly."

"I just got here, AJ."

"You know you want to."

"AJ!" Samara laughed. "You sound like a child!"

He shrugged and chuckled as well. "I'm quite possessive, Samara."

"Not making me want to come back to Athens."

"You like my possessiveness, *khriso mou*. You like me holding you close and kissing you. You like the fact I don't ever want to let you go. Don't you, Samara?"

She cleared her throat. "That is...um...rather nice."

"Then come home so I can do all those things and more."

"More?"

Her voice was husky and it made him grow hard. "Yes, Samara. A whole lot more. Would you like to know what the 'more' is?"

"No."

"Liar."

She sucked her teeth. "You only want me for my body!"

He laughed, imagining her face scrunched up into a pout. "That's not true. I want you for your heart and soul as well. We're mates, and I don't mean friends, although we're that too. We're soulmates, Samara, and you know it."

"AJ—"

"But I'll give you this time," AJ promised, aware that just because he was ready, he couldn't force her to be. They were both young. He could wait, especially since he knew for whom he was waiting. By the end of the year they would be together. That was a guarantee.

NINE

The intervening four months were full of late nights and daydreams, at least for AJ. He and Samara would speak for hours on the phone; and when funds were tight, they would instant message each other. Samara sent pictures via e-mail of them together as well, courtesy of Frankie, and AJ printed them and put one in a frame on his nightstand. It was of them at sunset on the *Isis*. Apparently, Frankie had snapped it while they dozed.

He and Samara had also invested in webcams, and during conversations that became reminiscent of their time on the yacht, they shared their mutual desire for each other through the tiny lenses. Though there was temporary relief, it still wasn't good enough.

Sooner than anticipated, it was Christmas. While it was normally among his favorite holidays, he felt an ache because Samara wasn't by his side. She and Frankie had sent him and Spyros authentic Philly cheesesteaks as gifts.

He had to see her.

Which was why he was standing in the airport terminal, nervous and trying desperately not to show it, while his mother and cousin watched him. He was going to surprise Samara for the New Year. It had seemed like a good idea at three in the morning when he'd impulsively bought the ticket to New York. She'd said she was spending the holiday with Frankie in the city and they were experiencing it as tourists despite the fact Frankie was a junior at Columbia. The university was closed for winter break, so they were staying at a local hotel and visiting all the sites neither woman had the time to do while at work or going to classes. AJ had thought it was a great idea and had given the sisters two tickets to a popular Broadway musical for Christmas. Well, he and Spyros had. The Greek wine he'd promised Samara before and AJ's personal gift to her was in his luggage.

"Do you think this will work?" Spyros asked.

"I hope so."

"*Esta es muy romántica, hijo,*" Luz said. AJ smiled and kissed her cheek.

"And hopefully Dimitri doesn't mess this up."

"His mother would kill him," AJ told Spyros confidently. "That, and it could only help him in the long run to help me."

Both cousins smirked. Their American cousin was having his own difficult time with his woman.

A quick rap to the back of the head had them both exclaiming and wincing. "Behave," Luz chided them in Greek.

"Yes, ma'am."

Spyros and Luz stood behind the roped-off queue as AJ went to the counter and checked in his luggage. When he left the counter, boarding pass in hand, he approached his mother and kissed her cheek again.

"I'll call when I touch down in New York."

"Say hello to Dimitri for me," Luz said and Spyros nodded in agreement.

"I will."

With a final hug to his mother and cousin, AJ walked through the security check and to his gate. With him was a book Samara had recommended he read, *The Sea-Wolf* by Jack London, a story he hadn't read yet. "I'll admit it's been a while since I've read it myself," Samara had said, "but I think you'll enjoy it."

He hadn't gotten far in the book, and his flight wouldn't take off for another hour, so he decided to make more headway into it. Also in his bag were more Samara recommendations: *Of Mice and Men*, by John Steinbeck; *As I Lay Dying*, by William Faulkner; and poetry by Paul Laurence Dunbar.

"What are you reading, handsome?"

AJ looked up to see a stunning redhead woman with smooth, alabaster skin; bright, blue eyes; and perfectly bee-stung pink lips grinning at him. A dusting of freckles on her bare shoulders added to her attractiveness. Her hair was a heavy, wavy curtain draped over one shoulder, clearly meant to entice. If there were no Samara, he would've been.

Returning her smile, AJ showed her the cover of the book, and she appeared to nod in approval. "Do you like it so far?"

"I've not been displeased."

The woman's smile widened, and she held out a hand. "Noelle."

AJ used the index finger of his left hand as a bookmark and shook Noelle's hand with his right. "AJ."

"A strong grip," Noelle said, her blue eyes looking at their joined hands briefly before meeting his gaze again. "Nice."

AJ smiled again and eased his hand from hers. "Thanks."

It was odd not having the desire to flirt. He felt decidedly out of his element. Flirting had been second nature, like breathing to him, before Samara. He'd even flirted with Dimitri's woman when she'd been in Greece. Now, all he wanted to be was left alone with the book Samara insisted he read. He knew the woman was interested in him, but AJ didn't know how to tell her he wasn't—he'd never had to do such a thing before.

"Leaving or going?" Noelle asked.

He blinked at the text in confusion before turning his green eyes to her. "Sorry?"

"Home. Leaving or going? Although I hear a faint accent, so I'm assuming leaving."

He smiled genuinely as an image of Samara appeared in his mind. "Going. Definitely going."

"Hmm. Greece didn't do it for you? I personally love it here. It's a shame I have to go back. I could live here," Noelle revealed.

AJ hoped Samara felt the same way. "It's easy to fall in love. Where did you visit?" Uninterested or not, he loved speaking about his homeland.

They started talking, and he found how easy it was to have a conversation with a woman and not be attracted to her. Though he appreciated Noelle for the classic beauty she was, it didn't go beyond aesthetic. And Noelle seemed to be as classy as she was beautiful, for she had gathered he wasn't interested in her in any other way than as a tourist who'd fallen in love with his country.

"It's a shame you're taken," Noelle said, bringing him up short as he spoke of other sailing routes e outside the Saronic Gulf.

"What?" He'd never told her his relationship status.

Noelle smiled and shrugged. "Am I lying?"

AJ knew he was blushing, more caught off guard than anything else. "How did you guess?"

"Because you keep mentioning this 'Samara' woman so often I can't help but notice. Wife?"

He licked his lips and let the corners of his mouth quirk. "Not yet."

Noelle turned fully in her seat to face him. "Oh, I love a good romance. How long have you known each other?"

"A few months."

"How did you meet?"

AJ began telling the story, mildly surprised how easily it fell from his lips. Noelle sat listening with rapt attention as he spoke, and he had only reached the day when they'd been in the National Garden before the boarding announcement sounded.

Noelle pouted and checked her boarding pass. "Darn, I'm not done listening. Where are you sitting?"

"Business class," AJ said. He never could stomach sitting economy on international flights.

Noelle's eyes widened. "That's great! I'd upgraded on a whim today, 14C. Decided to treat myself."

"Was your travel for pleasure?" AJ asked.

Noelle smiled and shook her head. "Job. I work as a museum curator, and I was trying to broker a deal with one of the smaller museums in Athens."

"How did it go?"

"Fingers are still crossed. We might get an answer later today or tomorrow," Noelle said. "Come, let's see how close we're sitting. I want to finish hearing the story!"

Turned out they were sitting two rows apart, with her behind him. Noelle managed to convince the man who had originally been sitting next to him to swap seats with her, and AJ had looked at her with amusement.

"What?" Noelle said innocently, twiddling her fingers at the man who smiled and nodded back. "I think a date with me isn't a bad tradeoff at all."

"Even though he's old enough to be *my* father?"

Noelle shrugged and winked. "Maybe he has a son?"

AJ laughed and nodded. "Okay, so where was I?"

"Her sister and your cousin had just left to go to the Zappeion."

"Oh, right," AJ said, an automatic smile blooming on his face at the memory. He started telling the story again, only pausing when they had to listen for announcements or when Noelle asked a question. He didn't know how long he spoke; but when he'd finished, he looked around the cabin and saw many people were taking naps or watching movies. The little map that showed the plane's progress on its journey showed it was well over the Atlantic Ocean.

"Forgive me," AJ said, flushing slightly. "I don't usually talk this much."

"No, it's okay," Noelle said sincerely, her smile soft and wistful. She was curled in her seat facing him, her pale, slender hands underneath her cheek. "I never heard someone talk about a person he loved like you do. I thought people only spoke like that in movies."

AJ grinned, remembering Samara had said something similar about their portrait. He shrugged and winked at her. "Well, they have to get those things from somewhere."

Noelle smiled, her eyes sparkling and bright. "Do you have a picture of her?"

AJ nodded and reached underneath the seat in front of him for his wallet. He pulled out the photo of them on the sunset and showed it to her.

Noelle didn't say anything immediately, her eyes going from the photograph to him as they took on a look of astonishment. "Wow...AJ...I just...wow..."

AJ nodded as if in understanding. "I thought the same when I first saw her."

"And it only took you five days to figure it out?" Noelle, her voice full of wonder.

AJ shrugged. "Fewer."

"Well, she's...not who I expected, if I'm honest, but you two fit. She's lovely, AJ."

Part of AJ bristled at that, but he nodded, letting the first part of the comment slide. Spyros had thought the same and now he rooted for him and Samara almost as fiercely as AJ himself did.

Noelle nodded and yawned delicately, though her mouth curved into a smile. "I wish there were more men out there like you. American men seemed to have lost the flair for pretty words and romance...well, those who are sincere, anyway."

"Come to Greece more often," AJ said, his teasing tone belying the seriousness of his suggestion. "We're fantastic men."

"And yet your Samara still got on the plane to come back to the States?" Noelle murmured sleepily, her eyes drooping.

The question echoed inside AJ's mind, but he didn't bother to answer, both because he didn't know and because Noelle had fallen asleep. AJ asked the flight attendant for a blanket as he passed. Once in hand, he draped the blanket over Noelle.

Samara had to come back to America. He knew that now. Everything had happened so quickly, too quickly for either of them to be ready for it. While he knew who Samara was and what she meant for him and his life, he'd been woefully unprepared to back up the promises and declarations he'd made inside his mind. They hadn't even I love yous to each other yet. He should've told her before she boarded the plane, should've put himself out there and trusted she wouldn't break his heart. Instead, he'd allowed her doubts to overcome them both.

But he was rectifying that now. He checked the plane's progress, and they were closer to North America than Europe. Only a few more hours, and he would be mere miles away from Samara instead of thousands. Glancing to Noelle again, he smiled. She had a brilliant idea. Maybe a nap would make the time go by faster.

He woke up to shaking, and he bolted upright, thinking the plane was experiencing a heavy bout of turbulence. When his mind finally caught up with his surroundings, he saw a grinning Noelle bent over him and the cabin lights fully illuminated.

"We've landed," she said, tilting her chin toward the window. Indeed, the airport was outside as the plane taxied to the gate. He relaxed in his chair and let a smile appear on his face.

Soon.

"Thinking about her?" Noelle asked.

AJ's smile widened.

So did Noelle's. "Think she thinks about you as often?"

"Hope so," AJ said. "Or else I'll feel incredibly foolish making this trip to see her!"

Once the plane reached the gate and the "Fasten Seatbelt Sign" went off, AJ unbuckled his belt and reached underneath the seat for his bag. He checked to make sure he had everything. Once satisfied, he stood and put his bag in the seat before reaching above to the overhead and grabbing Noelle's bag. He smiled at her soft, "thank you."

"Have a good day!" the flight attendants chirped when they disembarked the plane. Noelle and AJ kept chatting as they went to baggage claim. She was telling him of the sights he and Samara should see during his stay in the city. Apparently, the holiday season in New York was something to behold.

Though AJ's luggage came out first, he remained to help Noelle procure hers.

"Thank you so much," Noelle said again, touching AJ's elbow as he pulled her suitcases from the conveyor belt. "Samara's a damn lucky woman."

"I am the lucky party in this arrangement," AJ corrected sincerely. "Definitely the lucky one."

"AJ!"

Noelle and AJ turned to the sound of the voice, surprised they could hear it above the chattering of the baggage claim area. A large smile formed on AJ's face once he realized who it was.

"Cousin!" In a light mood, AJ went to his kin and lifted him off his feet, kissing both cheeks.

"Aw, c'mon, man!" his cousin cried indignantly.

AJ laughed and set the shorter man down. "You're heavy!"

"Nothing but muscle," he muttered in reply, then turned interested, yet sharp eyes toward Noelle. "This isn't Samara."

"No, it's not."

His cousin extended a hand to Noelle. "I'll excuse my cousin for his lack of manners. I'm Dimitri," Dimitri Melonakos said with a smile and slight bow.

"And I am single," Noelle said, definite approval in her eyes. "Noelle Schumacher."

"So is Dima."

"Slight technicality," Dimitri said, grimacing.

"Technicality?" Noelle asked.

Dimitri and AJ shook their heads wearily and Noelle chuckled, nodding. "Well, I hope things work out."

AJ laughed also and kissed Noelle's cheek. "And I hope 14C has a young, wealthy, attractive son waiting for you."

"I do too!" Noelle winked and went to the taxi stand where 14C was waiting.

AJ and Dimitri watched the gentle sway of her hips in platonic and aesthetic appreciation until she went out of sight. As if perfectly choreographed, they turned to each other and smiled.

"Makes you want to get on your knees and thank God, doesn't it?" Dimitri murmured.

"And you thought that was good? Samara's walk..." AJ took a moment of silence to think about it.

Dimitri scoffed and took hold of AJ's bag as if by habit. "You can't possibly mean to imply hers is better than Landi's."

A slow grin formed on AJ's face at the thought of Ilanderae Rouge Nycks—the bane of Dimitri's existence and his ladylove. "As succulent as Landi's walk is, I have to give the edge to Samara."

Dimitri's scowl had AJ laughing and giving a teasing buss to his forehead.

"Oy! C'mon! We're grown men now!" Dimitri wiped his forehead dramatically.

"You really need to be more secure in your manhood," AJ tsked, and skipped out of Dimitri's reach when the younger man tried to punch him.

"Why am I helping you foist yourself on someone who appears to be a very nice lady? Did she commit a felony?"

AJ made a rude gesture with his hand in response.

"And you made reservations at her hotel too? You realize this is borderline stalkerish?"

"Why *are* you here if you're going to be a pain in my ass?"

Dimitri stopped walking and blinked innocently. "Because you asked for my help and you love me?"

AJ growled low in his throat, cursing the fact Dimitri was right. Then he raised an eyebrow at his cousin. "And you aren't doing the same thing with Landi?"

Dimitri started walking again, going ahead of AJ and out of the airport. "This isn't about me."

AJ snorted. "How's she doing, by the way?"

Dimitri muttered under his breath as he led the way to their ride.

The traffic was atrocious, and it made AJ more anxious than he'd been while flying. Dimitri played a Dave Brubeck CD the sleek rental he drove. For the first thirty minutes, it was the only sound in the vehicle.

"How is Auntie?" AJ asked in Greek.

"Fine. She's wondering if you'll visit her while in the States," Dimitri replied in Greek as well, his tone absent as he focused on the road.

AJ's eyes widened. "Isn't she on the other side of the country?"

Dimitri shrugged, his strong fingers tapping on the steering wheel. "You know how Mother is."

"A wonderful woman."

Dimitri glared at him mildly. "You only say this because she's not *your* mother!"

"I'm sorry, have you met *my* mother?"

Both men shuddered.

Dimitri asked about AJ's mother, as well as Spyros, Anatole, and the other branches of the Melonakos tree. AJ told him of all the happenings—some important, most not—and the cousins shared laughter and somber moments as they filled in the blanks of recent Melonakos family history. For a second, there seemed to be a break in the traffic, and Dimitri put his foot on the gas, only to slam it on the brake when a driver from the left lane cut in front of him. AJ bit his lip as Dimitri railed in Greek at the inconsiderate driver.

"I see you're still fluent in those swear words I taught you," AJ said lightly.

Dimitri clenched his jaw and ignored him.

It was a sunny day, the kind that provided an illusion of warmth although AJ remembered seeing his breath when they'd walked outside to the vehicle. There wasn't snow on the ground, which was a bit disappointing, but there was a pulse in the large city that made his adrenaline pump.

The hotel Samara and Frankie had chosen was near Times Square. The rates were ridiculous to him; but considering it was the heart of the city and New Year's, AJ figured he was getting a steal compared to other places he could stay. Dimitri pulled up to the front of the hotel, whispering a prayer of thanks for the valet services, and the porter took out their luggage while the men went inside to the lobby. Dimitri had made the arrangements since he had a military discount, and it wasn't long before they had access to their room.

Two double beds occupied the space, as well as a television, writing desk, extra chair, and safe. Opening the closet, he also saw an iron and ironing board along with extra pillows and blankets.

"Nice," Dimitri said.

"Do you plan on staying here?"

"Only if Plan A doesn't work."

AJ nodded in understanding. Dimitri was here not only to help AJ win Samara, but also to help himself and his own love life. His woman lived not too far from the hotel, so he was going to surprise her on New Year's Eve. To help with that, AJ had arranged a romantic dinner at one of New York's finest restaurants and a Broadway play for them to see—his way of telling his cousin thanks.

Plan B, apparently, was for Dimitri to get all caveman-like and lock her in her home until someone gave in—that "someone" being her.

The men got settled, AJ reclining in the bed he'd claimed and calling his mother. He passed the phone to Dimitri so he could speak to his aunt, while Dimitri passed his own mobile to him so he could speak with Dimitri's mother.

"Nephew," Airlia Melonakos said, her Greek accent still apparent despite the many years she'd been in the United States. "I was starting to think you didn't love your aunt anymore, with you not calling and visiting for so long!"

Dimitri and AJ winced at each other before they went back to their conversations with their respective aunts.

"Things have been busy, Auntie," AJ spoke in Greek. "I apologize, but I will make a trip out there special to see you next time I'm in the country."

"Hmm, and who is this girl you are trying to make a Melonakos? Is she Greek?"

AJ blushed and rubbed the back of his neck, chuckling silently as he saw Dimitri flush and pull at the collar of his shirt. "No, *theia*. She is American."

"Oh," Airlia said, mildly disappointed. "Is she beautiful?"

"Almost as beautiful as you."

She made a clucking sound with her tongue. "Charmer." She laughed. "You Melonakos men…"

"You love us, *theia*," AJ said with a warm smile, spying his reflection in the turned-off television set.

"To your benefit," Airlia said primly. "I expect to see you soon, Alejandro, along with your woman. And my *gios*? Help him with his, though I've yet to meet her, either."

"I will, *theia*, I love you," AJ said with sincerity.

"You, too, *anepsios*. Make sure Dimitri gets back on the phone," she said.

Dimitri was finishing his conversation as well, and they passed the phones back to each other.

"Hello, Mama," they said at the same time before falling into their personal discussions.

"Both of my boys *enamorados*," Luz murmured, and AJ imagined her smiling softly.

"Yes, Mama," AJ said with a smile of his own. All of their mothers treated each son as if he was theirs. Luz was particularly this way because she'd only had one child. The other Melonakos women had had multiple. Even when Dimitri's family had moved to the States, they'd always been close. Of course, as they grew older, individual lives had gotten in the way; but this was a time for fresh starts and new beginnings, and what better way to do that than to add wives to it?

"I cannot wait to meet both women, properly this time," Luz mildly chastised.

"You will. I guarantee it. And Spyros hasn't burned down the restaurant, has he or Anatole?"

"*Ten más fe en tus primos, hijo*," Luz reprimanded.

"*Lo siento*, Mama," AJ said genuinely. "I know they will do fine."

"Yes, they will."

"I'll let you go to bed; it's late over there," AJ said and he kissed into the receiver. "*Te amo*, Mama."

"*Te amo, hijo*. Call me tomorrow, okay?"

"I will. Say hello to everyone else for me."

"*Sí, sí, ciao*," Luz said, then hung up the phone. AJ closed his mobile and lay on his bed atop the covers. He still wore his shoes, though his limbs hung well enough off the bed.

Dimitri hit his feet, dodging out the way as AJ attempted to kick him. "You can be so bloody annoying."

"And you can be an asshole, doesn't mean I love you any less," Dimitri teased, sitting on the edge of AJ's bed. "Gonna take a nap?"

"I'm exhausted."

Dimitri nodded and swiped a hand along his jaw. "I'll make some calls, get things in order. Want to go out to eat tonight?"

"We have to. This place doesn't have room service, does it?"

"Good point. Will six be all right?"

AJ draped an arm across his eyes and nodded. "Call me if your plans change?"

Dimitri laughed and slapped AJ's knee. "If they change, I hope I'm too *busy* to call!"

AJ groaned and shoved Dimitri's hand off. "Cad! No wonder why she—" A forceful hit to the shin cut off the rest of AJ's speech and he hissed.

"Behave, cousin," Dimitri warned.

AJ did, mainly because he was too tired to challenge Dimitri.

"I'll be back at 1700 hours, 1730 at the latest."

AJ waved haphazardly in the direction of Dimitri's voice, his body already succumbing to slumber. It was dreamless, nothing but a warm, heavy cloak of black so he could fully rest. At some point, he'd managed to toe off his shoes and burrow under the covers. He didn't know how long he'd slept; but when he awoke, the red numbers on the alarm clock red five after five and there was no sign of Dimitri. Suddenly antsy again, AJ slid on his shoes and grabbed his keycard before leaving his room. He wanted to get a better layout of the hotel briefly before having dinner. He went around his floor, past the elevator bank to where the ice and vending machines were. He'd exchanged his money at a travel agency before he left Athens, knowing he'd get the better deal there, but he didn't have any cash on him, just checks, and of course his credit cards. Since they would eat soon, AJ didn't bother to covet one of the snacks inside the machine. He turned to go back to his room so he could freshen up.

"Dang! Got off on the wrong floor!"

His heart clenched as he heard the voice. He hurried towards the elevator banks and saw the woman press a brown finger on the "up" button on the wall. He stood there silently, watching her mumble under her breath and continuously press the button, as if that would beckon the elevator faster.

"I don't think that will work, but I could be wrong."

Gasping, she turned to face him, her eyes widening upon recognizing him. "AJ!"

He smiled slowly. "Fancy seeing you here."

TEN

Frankie stood there frozen, shocked, too shocked to realize the elevator had reached their floor. By the time she had, the elevator had closed and moved on. She huffed and cursed, pressing the button again before turning her attention back to AJ.

"AJ!"

"Yes." AJ chuckled, approaching her slowly. "Can I get a hug?"

"A hug?"

He winced and placed his hand over his heart. "You wound me, Frankie."

She rolled her eyes but gave him a sincere embrace. "What are you doing here!"

"Visiting my cousin."

"And you happened to be in the same hotel?"

"Fate."

Frankie snorted. "Right!" She pulled back and regarded him carefully. "Visiting a cousin...the American one? Is Spyros with you?"

"Miss him, do you?"

Frankie blushed and averted her gaze. "It was just a question."

"That's all right, I have a gift for you from him. He'd try to kill me if I didn't give it to you."

"Try!"

"As if he could succeed!" AJ laughed. "My mother would have his hide!"

Frankie grinned and shrugged, keeping better watch on the elevators this time. "Does Samara know you're here? She would've mentioned to it to me if she did, right?"

"No, she doesn't know, and please don't tell her."

Frankie turned her attention to him, her eyes widening. "A surprise! Oh, wow!"

"Hopefully."

"And just what's gonna happen to me while you're off 'surprising' her?"

"I'll admit I didn't give that much thought—"

"Thanks a lot!"

"But you live in the city, Frankie," AJ said. "You have friends here, I'm sure. Samara's older than you are; do you really think she wants to be with you and your friends during the New Year? What about her friends?"

"She's friends with them too!" Frankie said, breaking off the conversation so she could step into the newly arrived elevator. AJ followed but didn't enter, placing his hand on the door to keep it open.

"Look, I know I made a huge gamble coming here, even a selfish one, but I let your sister go once. I'm not going to do it again."

"And just forget about her little sister—!"

"Why would you say that?" AJ asked. The doors tried to close, but AJ pushed them back and Frankie pressed a button AJ was sure was keeping the doors opened as well.

"If she goes with you, be it now or later, what about me?"

"What *about* you?"

Frankie gaped at him, then let go of the button. "Fine. I see you, I see you."

AJ stepped in the threshold of the elevator, uncaring the doors tried to squeeze him between them. "Is your sister happy, Frankie? Is she?"

Frankie's jaw clenched and she dropped her eyes from his.

"What room number are you?"

The mechanical whirring of the doors trying to close was starting to become bothersome, but he wouldn't leave until Frankie gave him the information he sought.

"Room 1132," Frankie said monotonously.

"We're 817," AJ informed her. "We're going to dinner at six, my cousin and I. Are you hungry?"

"We have the show at eight, something like that, but I'll talk to Samara. She was taking a nap when I left her."

AJ smiled, remembering the time they'd slept in each other's arms. "Don't wake her up because of it. I plan to see her soon. No hurry." Well, that last bit was a lie, but he could find a reserve of patience within him.

"Too kind," Frankie said, half-sarcastically, but AJ wasn't offended. He had come here to obliterate her plans with her sister; and while perhaps he should feel a bit guiltier about it, he didn't. Not at all.

He stepped back and let the doors close amid the bells creating a racket in his ears. Frankie huffed and crossed her arms over her chest, setting her eyes to the ceiling as if praying for strength. AJ chuckled, especially when the other elevator opened and out stepped Dimitri.

"Hey!" Dimitri said, a wide grin on his face. He slapped a hand on AJ's shoulder.

AJ chuckled. "Plan A is a go?"

"It is, even if she doesn't know it yet," Dimitri said, walking them down towards the room.

"You think it will work?" AJ asked. He opened the door with his keycard and both men stepped inside.

"I'm a Melonakos. When have we ever *not* gotten the woman of our dreams?"

It would certainly be a sad state of affairs if their generation of Melonakos men let the family name down, but Melonakos men were nothing if not determined and persistent.

"She won't be able to resist you," AJ said sincerely. "She might be angry, but no one who is smart allows anger to keep her from true love."

"True love..." Dimitri murmured almost dreamily. "At first sight."

"Yes," AJ said, thinking about when he first saw Samara at the market. "Instantaneous. Wonder why our women don't embrace it as fully as we do."

"Americans tend to shy away from things like that. With good reason. People are crazy in this country," Dimitri said with a grave shake of his head.

"Which is undoubtedly why you fit in well here, cousin!"

"I'm telling Mama!" Dimitri announced. "You called her crazy!"

"I called *you* crazy," AJ said, getting his cousin in a loose headlock and tackling him onto a bed. The cousins roughhoused for a few before Dimitri got the upper hand, not nearly as breathless as AJ was.

"I win," Dimitri said smugly.

"I let you win," AJ muttered, though he couldn't help but be proud of his cousin's rightful victory. Seemed the American Navy had benefited him greatly. "Besides, I have to go shower."

"Just as soon as you say I won fairly," Dimitri asked, pressing AJ further into the mattress.

His arrogance would be his downfall, AJ mused, and he bucked hard, surprising Dimitri so much he tumbled off AJ to the bed before rolling onto the floor.

"*Ow!*"

"Sorry, cousin," AJ said as sincerely as he could while holding in his laughter. He went around the bed and helped Dimitri stand. Dimitri glowered at him and AJ mussed his hair affectionately.

Dimitri muttered not-so-nice things in Greek and shoved AJ towards the showers. "You stink!"

"Love you too," AJ said cheekily, and he went to his suitcase and pulled out underwear and clothes before going into the shower.

He washed quickly, far too anxious to go downstairs and possibly meet Samara. He toweled off and slipped on his boxers, then shaved and brushed his teeth. He sprayed on a light, woodsy cologne and combed his hair, though there wasn't that much to comb since he'd gotten a haircut before leaving Athens. He felt like a teenager going on his first date instead of a thirty-four-year-old man who had gone on multiple. This was important to him, however; and though he and Samara had been communicating all the while, it had been months since they'd physically been in each other's presence.

He stepped out to find Dimitri hadn't changed; but as he hadn't been flying for hours straight, there hadn't been a need for him to do so.

"Ready?" Dimitri asked, clipping his pager and mobile to his belt. He shoved his wallet in the pocket of his khakis. His black polo shirt accentuated his fitness despite Dimitri's casual look. The Melonakos men were broad by nature, but Dimitri's Navy training had defined his more.

"I look all right?"

Dimitri smiled and nodded, as if seeming to understand his opinion was important to AJ's peace of mind. "You look almost as good as I do, cousin."

AJ smiled as well, clapping Dimitri's shoulder as they left the room. "You'll love her, Dima."

"Sorry, I'm already taken."

AJ laughed and shoved Dimitri away from him. Dimitri, also laughing, kept ahead of him and pressed the down button to the elevators once they reached the elevator bank. They said nothing as they waited for the car, both lost in thought. AJ could feel his upper lip start to bead with sweat, and he swiped his hand over his mouth absently. Would Samara like him clean shaven? Granted, a goatee wasn't a beard, but he'd had it for so long. It had been a random, almost rash decision one morning before the holidays as he'd been tightening up the goatee. His mother had loved it, framing his face and squeezing his cheeks in a manner she hadn't done since he was a child.

"You have a beautiful mouth, *mijo*. It's about time your mama got to see it again!" Luz whispered, right before placing a maternal kiss on said mouth. The sentiment encouraged him, even if it was his mother's opinion. Just the thought of Samara placing her soft hands on his smooth cheeks and kissing him in a far less motherly way...

"You're blushing," Dimitri said with amusement. The elevator arrived and the men got inside. AJ was thankful they were alone.

"I'm a little warm," AJ said gruffly and rolled his shoulders as he clasped his hands in front of him. Dimitri's cough didn't mask his chuckle. "Shut up."

"You're a goner."

"So are you," AJ said, and the elevator opened upon reaching the lobby. He didn't see Frankie or

Samara there, so they sat on one of the couches provided. He shouldn't be nervous, but AJ couldn't help it. After months of a virtual Samara, the ability to hold her in his arms had him anxious to do so.

Dimitri tapped his biceps after a few minutes had passed, pulling AJ's attention from his feet to the check-in desk.

"Is that her?" Dimitri asked.

AJ shook his head. "No, her sister. Come, I'll introduce you."

The pair stood and approached the desk. Frankie was nodding at something the receptionist was saying. Gently, AJ touched Frankie's shoulder so he wouldn't startle her, but she jumped anyway.

"Way to go, AJ," Dimitri said dryly, rolling his eyes.

"I'm *sayin'*!" Frankie muttered, slapping AJ's chest. "Scarin' people!"

"Sorry," AJ murmured, genuinely contrite. "I just wanted to say hello and introduce you to my cousin. Frankie, this is Dimitri. Dimitri, this is Frankie, Samara's sister."

As he had with Noelle, Dimitri bowed, except this time he pressed a gallant kiss upon the back of Frankie's hand. Frankie's eyes fluttered a bit, and AJ saw the definite beginnings of a blush.

"Hmm," Frankie said, once Dimitri relinquished her hand. "Maybe I *do* need to move to Greece."

"Spyros misses you," AJ said with a wink.

Dimitri scowled. "Oh, *no!* She's *far* too lovely to saddle with Spyros!"

Frankie's blush intensified, and AJ laughed. "He wanted to come, but he had to mind the restaurant."

"So you brought another cousin to keep me occupied," Frankie said, raising an eyebrow. "Think you slick."

"Not like that at all. Dimitri's trying to make his own love connection—"

"And thank you, CNN," Dimitri said with a glare.

Frankie laughed, and the men smiled at her. AJ couldn't wait to make her his sister-in-law.

Speaking of..."Are you coming with us to dinner, or is Samara still taking a nap?" If she were, AJ would try his best not to be disappointed.

"Oh, actually I was about to go get some soup for her," Frankie said. "Apparently she's not feeling very well. I checked if she had a fever, but she didn't feel warm."

AJ's heart clenched. "What happened? Did she take anything—?"

"Maybe the lunch we had didn't agree with her," Frankie said with a shrug. "She had a hotdog."

"From a street vendor?" Dimitri asked, as if aghast. "Even *I* know better than to—!"

AJ and Frankie frowned at him, and he closed his mouth.

"Would you like me to get the soup for you?" AJ asked, his mind fixated on Samara and whatever he could do to help her feel better quickly.

"No, I know where to get some, but...you want to stay with her?"

Relief almost made him sag, and he kissed Frankie's forehead. "Bless you. I'll stay until you come back."

"And I'll go with you," Dimitri said to Frankie. When Frankie gave him a look that clearly said she could walk the streets of New York alone, and *had* many times, Dimitri gave her a lopsided grin. "It would make me feel better."

"He's Navy," AJ said, as if that explained everything.

Frankie rolled her eyes. "Whatever."

Dimitri nodded. "I'll wait here while you two go back upstairs. I hope she feels better soon. I'd like to meet the woman who has my cousin's heart."

With a nod towards Dimitri, AJ and Frankie went back upstairs to her and Samara's room. Frankie knocked on the door softly before unlocking it with her key and stepping inside. There were two double beds, and AJ saw the outline of Samara's body beneath the covers of one of them. She was facing away from the door curled into a semi-fetal position, and her arms hugged the pillow beneath her head.

"Sam?" Frankie asked, her voice barely above a whisper. Samara didn't budge. AJ stepped further into the room, his eyes never leaving Samara.

"Don't wake her," AJ whispered. "You should probably go ahead and get the soup."

"Okay."

It was only after he heard the door close with Frankie's exit that he approached Samara's bed. He went into the space between the beds, bracing himself against the nightstand as he crouched down so he could be level with her. He pressed his hand on her cheek, glad to find she still wasn't warm, but his thumb began a caress. Her brows furrowed a little, and he kissed it away.

"I'm here, my love, I'm here."

Her frown deepened, and she tilted her head so more of her face was in his hand. Seconds later, those brown eyes of hers opened, clearly unfocused and full of disbelief.

"Samara?"

"Didn't you have a goatee a minute ago?"

AJ smiled, resuming his thumb's caress against her cheek. "Did I?"

She blinked at him, pursing her lips. "You weren't wearing a blue shirt, either. It was green. And short-sleeved—"

She sat up abruptly, then brought her hands to her head to cradle it. AJ cupped the back of her head and whispered softly against her temple in Greek. Soon, her body began trembling, and AJ scooted closer to the bed to hold her tighter.

"AJ?"

"Yes, my love," AJ replied, his own body starting to tremble. Samara pulled back, her eyes wide with incredulity and tears.

"AJ?"

"Samara," he answered, internally, desperately, trying to convince himself it wouldn't do for him to start blubbering along with Samara.

Unsteady fingers reached up to caress his mouth. Unable to help himself, AJ kissed the digits as they skimmed his lips, and Samara let out a sob.

"Oh, God…"

He hugged her then, more because he couldn't go another second without her fully in his arms, and partly because her sob had caused two tears to slip from his eyes. The restlessness he'd been feeling all day—nay, the last four months—suddenly dissipated now that he could hold her, smell her, feel her.

She buried her face in the crook of his neck, and her breath against his skin really made it sink in that she was breathing and in his embrace. He wasn't dreaming, as Samara had been just moments before. This was real, oh, so real.

"*S'agapo*, Samara."

She tensed, as if she instinctively knew what he'd just said. Admittedly, he hadn't meant to tell her that this way. It would've been during a romantic date, after a wonderful dinner, and while they leisurely strolled through Central Park with arms wrapped around each other to keep away the chill. He would have tipped her head back, looked deep into her eyes, and told her of his love.

Yet here, with her not feeling so great, and both of them clinging to each other frantically, his heart had forced its feelings out before another moment could pass between them. That she was still silent didn't bother him as much as it should've; perhaps she thought she was still dreaming. He'd been in one from the moment he'd met her.

"AJ?"

He chuckled. His name seemed to be the only thing she could say aside from her brief supplication to the Lord. "Yes, my love. I am here."

Her fingers curled into the nape of his neck. She took a deep breath and AJ kissed her temple again before laying her back in the bed. She looked at him as he tucked her in, tears still in her eyes, and she shook her head.

"You're not really here..."

AJ smiled and kissed her forehead. "I'm here. With you. Taking care of you. Rest up, Samara. You've got to be feeling well for the New Year."

She nodded, dazedly acquiescing to his logic. AJ waited until her eyes fell shut before he went to the other side of the bed and climbed in with her. He took off his shoes but remained atop the covers just in case she would need something. He draped an arm around her waist and smiled more when she scooted back against him, as if unconsciously. Her hair, still short, was soft when he brushed a palm over it before slipping that arm underneath her neck to hold her close. Though he'd already taken a nap and his stomach desperately wanted nourishment, he didn't want to be anywhere else than here.

AJ fell asleep again, his body not adjusted to the time change yet. He felt himself getting a rest it hadn't received in months. He was completely relaxed, and it was almost as if he could feel his body repair its wear and tear. It was the physical manifestation of being truly carefree. He didn't wake up until he was nudged, and he opened his eyes to see Dimitri and Frankie watching them. Immediately, AJ checked on Samara, who had snuggled into his body with her cheek resting against his shoulder and her arm slung around his middle.

AJ smiled.

"She's comfortable," Frankie noted.

"She should be," AJ agreed and kissed the top of Samara's head.

"We have soup," Dimitri added, holding up the paper bag with the meal. "Chicken noodle. Got a sandwich for you. Roast beef."

AJ nodded. "Thank you." Dimitri set it on the dresser opposite the beds while Frankie sat on her bed. Dimitri sat beside her, and the three of them said nothing as AJ watched Samara sleep. "I'd given her some Pepto," Frankie said, "and told her to rest."

"Yeah, she woke up for a minute. I don't think she thinks I'm here," AJ said, grinning at them.

"She thinks you're something, the way she's wrapped all over you," Frankie said, grinning in return.

"A pillow," Dimitri supplied with a dry expression.

"I don't mind it. Not at all," AJ admitted and held Samara closer.

AJ noticed Frankie checking the clock on the nightstand and she sighed. "Well, I guess we won't be going to Broadway."

"Why do you say that?"

"The tickets you got us—thanks, by the way—are for tonight, an hour and a half from now. She's not gonna be feeling well, and I don't want to go alone."

"I'll go with. What show?" Dimitri said, looking between Frankie and AJ. "My plans don't go into effect until tomorrow anyway, and since I think AJ would be more than happy to stay with your sister."

Frankie bit her lip and glanced at Samara. "She *really* wanted to see it."

"She will," AJ promised. "Go have some fun, Frankie. I plan to take care of your sister for the rest of her life. May as well start now."

Frankie gaped at him, then looked to Dimitri for confirmation. "Is he serious?"

Dimitri nodded. "We Melonakos men never joke about our women."

"But—"

"You have a problem with me becoming your brother-in-law, Frankie?" AJ asked, running a hand along Samara's back idly. "Do you dislike me?"

"No! But—"

"No yelling," Samara mumbled, and buried her face into AJ's shoulder. "Headache."

AJ's attention snapped back to Samara, and he bent his mouth to her ear. "Love? Samara?"

She snuggled closer but said nothing.

"You should probably wake her anyway. Don't want the soup to get too cold," Frankie said. She stood and Dimitri followed. "Ready to babysit?"

"Nay, cousin, you are too much of a woman for anyone to babysit," Dimitri said, presenting the way to her.

"Cousin, huh?" Frankie said as she walked ahead of him.

"Like I said, we Melonakos men don't joke. He's serious about your sister, and God help any woman who thinks we aren't!"

With that, the door closed gently behind him, and AJ chuckled. He knew Dimitri was saying that as much for Frankie's benefit as for his own woman, hoping the universe would cosmically send the message to her before they met again.

AJ ran his knuckles along Samara's cheek. "God, I love you." He kissed the cheek he'd been caressing before leaving the bed and taking the food out the bag. The soup was still warm, perfect for her to eat soon, and he poured some in a bowl along with the saltines that were in the bag. If they'd been at home, AJ would've made her Avgolemono soup, the Greek version of chicken noodle soup except much better, in his humble opinion. He would have no problem taking complete care of her, either. He remembered his father taking three days from the restaurant to care for his mother when she'd gotten the flu. AJ had been nine at the time, and to see his tall, proud papa wait and worry over his mother had been amazing to him. AJ had even asked why he was doing "women's work," and AJ's papa had laughed shortly.

"Caring and devotion is not solely a woman's realm, *gios*," Kyriakos had said as he stirred a large pot of Avgolemono. "Your mother, I love that woman, and it is my duty as a man and a husband to make sure my wife is happy, healthy, cared for, and loved. If you can do all those things, *gios*, you are truly a man."

There had been mutual respect and love between his parents; and every time he'd seen them together, he'd thanked God for giving him such a wonderful example of what a relationship should be. In fact, his entire family was such an example. Of course, AJ wasn't so naïve to think there hadn't been wild periods among his father or uncles, and he was sure his own mother had had relationships before meeting his father. But after they'd found each other, that had been it. No more. There hadn't been a need to continue the search because they'd found their mates. He wondered if his parents had had that moment of doubt as he had—not that they weren't right for each other, but the insane fear something would break them up now that they'd found each other. Had they let each other go, as if to test the universe, or had they clung to each other and dare fate to tear them asunder?

AJ realized he should've asked his mother, but what did it matter? Thirty years of marriage was answer enough.

He looked around for a drink and didn't see any, but he did spy loose change beside the bag. He took it, promising himself to pay Frankie back, and then grabbed Samara's keycard and the ice bucket from the nightstand. He left the room and went down the hall where the ice and vending machines should be. He got an apple juice and filled the ice bucket with ice. When he returned, Samara was out of bed and staring at the food in confusion.

"Frankie, what is all...?"

They stared at each other, AJ hovering inside the doorway while Samara's mouth opened and shut as if she were just learning how to operate it. Never breaking eye contact, AJ left the doorway, the door closing automatically behind him. He dumped the juice and ice bucket next to the food absently, not caring that the apple juice rolled off the dresser and onto the floor. Samara, standing there in pajama shorts and a long-sleeved tee, tucked her hands in the hem of her shirt, as if unsure whether to flee or fly to him.

As soon as he was in striking distance, AJ took the decision away from her and hauled her against his chest. Before she could say a word, his lips covered her mouth, finally kissing her as he'd longed to do since before she'd gotten the plane and left Greece. Her arms wrapped around his neck, and his curled around her waist. Turning abruptly, his bum found the edge of the bed, and he lifted her so she straddled his hips. Her hands slid up the back of his head. Her fingers tangled in his hair. Her tears scaled his cheeks.

"*Shh*," AJ cooed, breaking their intense kiss to buss them away. "*Shh...*"

Samara, eyes closed, leaned her forehead against his and cupped his cheek. "I thought..." She licked her lips, as if savoring his taste. "I thought I'd been dreaming."

AJ held her tighter and kissed her jaw. "I'm here, and I'm never letting you go again."

"Promise?"

"*Dikos mou orkos, mou zoi*," AJ whispered. "My vow."

Eleven

AJ fed Samara. It had been her idea to dump the lukewarm soup in the coffeepot and use the coffeemaker to warm it. His genius *agapi*. He definitely had to marry her now.

After he thought the soup was sufficiently warm, he poured it back into the bowl and handed it to her. Samara smiled her thanks.

He finished eating his roast beef sandwich before she was even halfway done with her soup. He monitored her progress for a while before he stood. "I'm going to go down to my room for a second, but I'll be back," he told her, smoothing his hand along her cheek.

"Yes, Dr. AJ," Samara teased, slipping a spoonful of soup into her mouth.

He chuckled. "I took your keycard earlier. May I borrow it again?" Samara nodded, and AJ kissed her forehead. "Be back soon."

"Okay."

He took the stairs, too anxious to wait for the elevators, and went into his room. He changed into his pajamas as well and picked up his book of Paul Laurence Dunbar poems and spare change before going back to Samara's room. He knocked before entering.

Samara smiled as brightly as she could around her spoon, her eyes reflecting her amusement. "Did this turn into a sleepover?"

"Do you mind?" AJ asked, sitting on the edge of the bed by her feet. He tweaked a toe that was underneath the covers and she chuckled.

"Why would I mind? I haven't seen you in months, you come all this way to see me...and you ask if I mind spending time with you? I just wish I didn't feel so crappy."

AJ rubbed her shin over the bedcovers. "Not feeling any better?"

"The food's staying down," Samara said, placing the empty bowl on the nightstand. It was good she ate all of it. Maybe she'd be feeling better tomorrow. "You know what time Frankie and your cousin will be back?"

AJ had told Samara they'd gone to see the show. "Maybe around ten-thirty or so. Don't worry. There's no better bodyguard she could have."

"I trust him," Samara said. "You trust him, I trust him."

AJ squeezed her foot. "Thank you." His throat strangely tight, he cleared it and held up the book. "Can I read to you?"

Samara smiled at him and laughed. "Read to me!"

AJ shrugged. "My father read to my mother when she wasn't feeling well. Of course, back then, we didn't have a television, but...if you want, obviously."

"I love the sound of your voice, AJ," Samara said softly. "This is really sweet of you."

He crawled up the bed, his body hovering over hers. Then he kissed her gently. He still tasted the broth on her lips, reminding him she was not well, and he pulled back reluctantly.

"I can read to you every night if you want. You don't have to be sick," AJ said.

"I feel better already."

"No doubt," AJ said, smiling slightly, "but I'm still not satisfied about your health."

"Dr. AJ," Samara said and nodded with a faux-serious expression.

AJ pecked her lips and then situated himself next to her on the bed. With one strong arm, he pulled her body until she sat between his legs, her back reclined against his chest. Both sighed with contentment.

"Did you have trouble with the vernacular?" Samara asked before he even started to read.

AJ grinned and nipped the curve of her ear, setting the keycard and Frankie's change on the nightstand. "I'll admit I had to sound some words out, but you can help me with those poems if you wish."

"It's a deal," Samara said and burrowed into him. AJ took a moment to just hold her, breathe in her scent. He could easily see them doing this every night before they went to bed.

"Okay, let's see," AJ said, resting his lips against her temple as he flipped through the book. He stopped on a poem called, "Night of Love". "This one good?"

"Perfect," Samara said.

One hand held the book open and the other rubbed Samara's tummy as he began to read. From then, his selections had been just as random as the first, though he had yet to read a poem he didn't like. He understood why she admired this poet. His work was diverse: witty, serious, melancholy, wistful, hopeful, provocative. If he found one with dialect, Samara would read to him instead. It was as if she became the speaker, able to convey the emotions behind the words and make him feel what the speaker did. Samara had said she loved the sound of his voice. Well, he adored hers.

Samara was helping him read "When Malindy Sings" when the door opened. Both were too engrossed in the reading and AJ stealing kisses along Samara's ears and cheeks to notice Frankie and Dimitri returning from the show. It wasn't until Dimitri shook the bed did they come to attention.

"Feeling better?" Frankie asked amusedly.

"Yes, ma'am," Samara said. AJ knew she was a little embarrassed, but she recovered well. "Hi, I'm Samara."

"And my cousin must've made a deal with the devil in order to have a woman as spectacular as you," Dimitri said, approaching the bed and bringing her hand to his lips. "Dimitri Melonakos at your service."

"And just what kind of service would that be?" AJ asked, noting the fact Dimitri had yet to release Samara's hand."

"Rescue, of course."

"He blows people up for a living, Samara, don't listen to him," AJ said, winking at Dimitri.

"What?" Samara asked.

"Navy SEAL, ma'am," Dimitri explained, glaring mildly at AJ. "He's just mad because he doesn't do anything exciting. Baking bread...how exhilarating!"

"Do not *mock* the family business, cousin—"

"And I thought you and Spyros were bad!" Frankie interjected, "banterin' all the time!" She plopped ungracefully onto her bed.

"Tired, boo?" Samara asked with older-sister concern. "Was the show good?"

"*Girl*, it was *fantastic*! AJ, those were great seats! We were so close, I think me and the lead had a moment..." Frankie fanned herself as if reliving said moment.

"Then I'm glad you didn't go," AJ whispered into Samara's ear. "I don't want you to 'have a moment' with anyone but me.!"

"Shush," Samara said, slapping AJ's knee lightly. "Did the songs sound as good as they do on the OBC soundtrack?"

"Better! You have to go. Are you sure you're feeling better?"

"AJ took excellent care of me," Samara said, and she earned a kiss on the cheek for her compliment. "But

I doubt I'll get to see it while on this trip. I go back to Philly on New Year's."

AJ locked eyes with Dimitri, who shrugged his shoulders imperceptibly. "Plans can change, *agapi mou*. You might get a chance to see it."

"Last-minute tickets? And tomorrow's New Year's Eve—?"

AJ kissed her silent, and she sighed into his mouth.

"That's one way of shutting her up," Frankie muttered.

Dimitri laughed.

"Jealous," Samara shot back, not even looking at her sister. AJ was glad she didn't feel ashamed of their display of affection.

"Meh, a little."

"Oh, I forgot to bring Spyros's gift. Tomorrow," AJ promised.

"'Kay," Frankie said, her eyes drooping shut. "Boy, I'm beat."

"Is that our cue, Miss Frankie?" Dimitri asked.

"Take it as you will," Frankie murmured, waving a hand lazily in the air.

Samara laughed and nuzzled AJ's neck. "I think little sis would like to go to bed now."

AJ nodded and kissed Samara's nose. His hand rubbed her soft belly. "Think I could convince her to let me stay?"

"No," said the other three in the room.

AJ laughed heartily and lifted his free hand in surrender. "Fine, I'll go." He tilted up Samara's chin and kissed her lips. "I don't want to leave."

"You'll see me tomorrow," she reminded him. "And in person, no less."

He kissed her again. "Well, then, let me hurry up and go to bed so tomorrow can come faster."

"Gag," Frankie mumbled.

"Seconded," Dimitri agreed.

"Jealous," AJ and Samara whispered, and kissed each other one last time. "Have a good night, Samara."

"You, too, AJ," Samara said. "Thank you for taking care of me."

"Always," AJ said, kissing the palm of her hand. He lifted Samara out his lap and slid out of bed, pressing his fingers to his lips in a final goodbye to her and waving at Frankie.

"Sweet dreams, ladies," Dimitri said, letting AJ out before him and closing the door gently behind them. The pair walked to the elevators silently. They didn't say a word until they reached their room. It wasn't until the door closed that Dimitri spoke again.

"She looks at you the way our mothers looked at our fathers," Dimitri murmured. "The way Landi used to look at me."

AJ clapped Dimitri's shoulder and squeezed. "I know. Why do you think I'm helping you get her back?"

"We're family."

"Yes," AJ said. "And that includes Landi, whether she wants to admit it or not." They said nothing else after that, both consumed with thoughts of the women they loved well into slumber.

The next morning, a knock on the door roused them. Dimitri, the earlier riser of the two, was more functional, having already showered and dressed, and he answered the door. It was a little after eight in the morning. AJ, still suffering from jetlag, lacked the energy to do anything but roll over and steal more shut-eye.

Moments later, he felt the bed dip, and he was more than ready to tell Dimitri to go away when he felt gentle lips upon his cheek.

He smiled. "*Frankie*...what would your sister say?"

"Meh, I've had better."

Amid Dimitri's whoop of laughter, AJ flipped Samara onto her back and gave her a thorough kiss. "Better than that?"

"I think I might need another kiss in order to make a fair judgment," Samara said, even as she brought his lips to hers. This time, AJ was gentler, savoring her taste of mint and fresh breath.

He winced in apology. "Does my breath stink terribly?" he asked, even if it seemed a little moot.

"I wouldn't complain if you brushed your teeth!" Samara laughed. She pressed her nose against his. "Good morning, AJ."

"Good morning, *agapi mou*," he murmured, kissing her forehead quickly before leaving the bed and going to the bathroom. He brushed his teeth quickly and washed his face.

"*Agapi mou*, what does that mean?" AJ heard Samara ask Dimitri.

"My love," Dimitri replied.

"Oh..." AJ heard Samara breathe. "What about, uh, *khriso mou*?"

"My precious one," Dimitri explained, then AJ heard him chuckle. "You're adorable when you blush."

"Cousin!" AJ said, coming out the bathroom and giving Dimitri a playful glare. "No flirting with my woman!"

"I'm merely stating a fact!" Dimitri said, wrapping his arm around Samara's shoulders. "Your woman is insanely adorable, actually, whether she blushes or not!"

"Y'all need to stop," Samara mumbled, averting her eyes and blushing even more.

AJ sat on the edge of his bed and tugged Samara to him. He kissed the palm of her hand, his eyes locked on her visage. "You're right, though, Dima," AJ said, his voice full of wonder. "She is adorable, and kind, and giving, and gorgeous...and mine."

Samara's eyes softened at his words, and she gave him a hug that he happily returned. "Are you hungry? Frankie and I are having breakfast. She should be down there now. I stopped by to see if y'all were awake and wanted to eat with us."

"Excellent plan," Dimitri said, kissing Samara's cheek. "I'll go down so Frankie doesn't feel lonely. AJ looks like he's interested in something other than a bagel."

"*Cousin*," AJ growled in warning, his thumb drifting over Samara's reddened cheek. Dimitri merely blew him a kiss and left the room.

"You two like to tease each other. All of you. You're close," Samara said after a few moments of silence.

"Brothers," AJ said. "Even if Dima's been in the States. We're brothers."

"The Melonakos are a close clan."

"Yes, we are," AJ affirmed, his thumb still caressing her cheek. "Do you approve?"

"How could I not? Who is a person without her family?" Samara said.

"And family is very important to you."

"Of course."

AJ nodded and brushed his mouth against hers. They needed to talk, but they would have plenty of time to do so. Right now, he was so hungry he could eat enough food for everyone in the hotel. "Come. Unlike what Dima said, a bagel would hit the spot right about now.

The sisters and the cousins shared a nice continental breakfast courtesy of the hotel. AJ did have his bagel and coffee while Dimitri had a bowl of mixed fruit and tea. Samara, not wanting to risk her stomach, also had fruit with more apple juice, and Frankie had cereal and water. Dimitri kept up a steady stream of conversation with Frankie about school and her semester thus far, while Samara focused on her meal and their discussion, and AJ focused on Samara. She seemed so proud of her sister, sometimes jumping in and answering before Frankie could. Frankie seemed annoyed by this, but obviously very used to it. AJ knew Frankie was glad she made Samara proud.

"She's going to be a professor. Tenured by thirty, you watch," Samara predicted.

"*Sam!*" Frankie hissed.

"What? You're the smart one in the family—"

"As if you're such an idiot!"

"I never said I *was...*"

"Well, she *did* choose my cousin—ouch!"

Dimitri rubbed the back of his head and scowled at AJ. AJ wouldn't apologize. He thumped the back of Dimitri's head in the stead of Auntie Airlia.

"No, it was the other way around," Samara admitted, suddenly shy again. "Apparently he had 'American girl' on his list of things to pick up from the market that day!"

"I did a squeeze test and everything," AJ said with a wink. Samara rolled her eyes.

"Oh! Sis, love," Frankie said, as if she had just been reminded of something. "A group of friends is meeting up at Central Park at around ten, and they wanted to know if I could come."

"Yeah, you don't need to ask my permission," Samara said, shrugging.

"But I know you wanted to do more sightseeing..."

"I can still go—"

"I'll be with her," AJ said, looking across the table where the two sisters sat. "And you still have my mobile."

"I do," Frankie said. "Cool, I'm gonna go, then. I'll check-in every now and again."

"Thank you," Samara said, smiling when Frankie squeezed her shoulder. "Y'all have a good day today and Happy New Year if I don't see you!"

They waved goodbye, and AJ's lips quirked when Dimitri scooted slowly from the table as well.

"Plans," Dimitri said simply, and AJ shook his hand.

"Good luck, cousin."

"Luck and prayer," Dimitri said with a sigh. "If all goes well, I won't see either of you until the New Year. Have an ecstatic one." He kissed Samara's hand.

"You, too, Dimitri," Samara said, her blush apparent. He winked at her and squeezed her hand, then released it and waved as he left them in the dining area. AJ looked across the table at her, and she met his gaze straight on.

"Just the two of us," AJ said, not the least bit disappointed by this turn of events.

"Apparently," Samara said with a little grin. "What would you like to do?"

"Loaded, so loaded a question, *agapi mou*."

Samara's blush overtook her entire face. AJ stood and helped her to her feet. Silently, he walked them to the elevator and held her close as they rode up to his floor. They went into his room, and AJ sat her on the bed.

"Feel free to turn on the television. I'll take a quick shower and change. I got some advice on places to visit."

Samara nodded, but instead of turning on the television, she picked up his copy of *The Sea-Wolf* and smiled.

"You got it," she said happily.

"I'm enjoying it," AJ told her.

"I'm glad. I loved Wolf."

AJ kissed her lips lightly. "I won't be long."

And he wasn't, taking an almost record shower, then putting on a fresh turtleneck and slacks. When he returned to the room, Samara was stretched out on his bed and reading the novel. Chuckling a little, AJ climbed into bed and kissed her cheek, earning a smile in response. "Want me to read this to you tonight?"

"It's New Year's Eve!"

"Oh, right."

"Do you want to go into Times Square?"

AJ had done it before during a business trip for the financial firm he'd been working for while in London, and he really didn't want a repeat. It was so crowded, and he was more afraid of getting separated from Samara and something happening to her. Yet if she wanted to go, he would.

"Do you?"

"You know I don't like crowds."

He curved an arm around her waist. "Then we won't go. Ready to go explore the city with me, *agapitos*?"

"Yeah." He noticed she hadn't lost his place in the book, and he smiled at her consideration. Hand in hand, they left his room and ultimately the hotel, deciding to go to Rockefeller Center first to see the tree, NBC Studios, and the Macy's Christmas window displays. Rarely did they let go of each other, his leather-gloved fingers interlaced with her wool-covered ones. There still wasn't snow; and while it wasn't frigid, it was colder than he preferred.

Truth be told, AJ spent more time looking at their reflection in the windows than at the displays. Samara seemed enthralled, and seeing the joy on her face made AJ's heart light and soul happy. She would point to things and gush over the ingenuity and overall cuteness of the window art; and as AJ looked around at the other couples and families enjoying the displays, he wondered if he and Samara would have a little Melonakos in a year's time doing this very thing. Eventually, they moseyed over to the ice rink and looked at the people skating. When AJ jokingly asked if she wanted to take a spin, Samara pinned him a look that told him he'd obviously lost his mind for suggesting it.

"Good, because I can't skate," AJ admitted sheepishly.

"No one's perfect," Samara said, squealing when he nipped at her neck playfully. It eventually led to a kiss and hug, and Samara's body curled into his.

"I'd forgotten how tall you are," Samara muttered as they pulled apart. "Is it uncomfortable for you?"

"Never," AJ said, wrapping his arms around her waist. "The furthest thing from it."

Samara rolled her eyes and smoothed her hands over the lapels of his leather jacket. It was a heavier version of the one he'd worn while she'd been in Greece. "You're a foot taller than I am, AJ."

"More of me to love," AJ said. "And if I really were concerned about the height, all I'd have to do is this—"

Samara swallowed a scream as AJ lifted her off her feet and kissed her again. She held onto him tightly. "Put me down!" she hissed.

"I actually rather like this," AJ mumbled against her lips. Samara glared at him. "Spoilsport." He slid her down the planes of his body, making sure she felt everything, especially his reaction to her. She didn't look at him as she turned around and started for Radio City Music Hall.

Naturally, it didn't take long for him to reach her, and he grasped her hand again. They spoke little as they walked up Avenue of the Americas, and AJ didn't mind it. Eventually, they found their way into Central Park, and their walk became a stroll. They followed the path with no real direction in mind; Samara hooked her arm through his and rested her head against his biceps. He kissed the top of her head.

"Want to take a break?"

"Okay."

They found an empty bench a few paces ahead, and they huddled together upon it. AJ took both of her hands in his as he watched the people walking along the path and beyond to the lake. Samara's eyes were closed.

"Do you still want to go to the party tonight?" AJ asked, brushing his lips against her temple. He knew Frankie and Samara had gotten tickets to attend the New Year's Eve party at Bryant Park Grill, but given Samara's health...

"Perhaps we should get you inside," AJ said, standing and bringing Samara to her feet. "I'm a fool keeping you out in the cold like this."

"I'm fine," Samara insisted.

"You were sick not twenty-four hours ago!" AJ said, angrier with himself. "I'm supposed to be taking care of you!"

"I'm a big girl," Samara reminded him. "You don't need to."

"You're *my* girl," AJ corrected. "And I damn well do!"

"And then when I leave tomorrow? You're gonna take care of me via webcam?"

"If you come to Greece with me, I won't need to!" AJ shot back.

Samara stopped short for a moment, then rolled her eyes and shook her head. "I can't—"

"Why not?" AJ said, grasping her elbows and bringing her to his chest. "Give me one good reason why you can't."

"You know why."

"I said *good* reason, Samara," he ground out, his green eyes narrowing dangerously. He wanted to shake her to get her to see she was hurting him and herself by not following her heart. A woman didn't kiss him like she did, touch him like she did, look at him like she did, if she weren't in love. "When will you stop putting yourself last?"

"I don't—"

"Do you even want to go to this party, Samara? You who are so shy and prefer peace to madness? You are going because Frankie wants to go!"

"I don't mind. What was I going to do other than sit on my couch and watch Dick Clark count in the New Year? Besides, it's dangerous for her to be here alone—"

"She has friends, Samara. She doesn't need a chaperone!" AJ said, loosening the hold he had on her arms.

"But our parents—"

"Need to realize Frankie is grown. So do you. So does Frankie. You're not her mother!"

"I never said I was!" Samara said, glaring at him. "But I'm the oldest..."

AJ nodded slowly. "And when you had fun with your friends? Who looked after you? Have you ever done a reckless thing in your life?"

"I fell in love with you! I think that's pretty damn reckless!"

It was as if the air had been sucked out the wintry afternoon. Samara dropped her eyes from his and stared at his chest. He had seen the tears starting to form, and he brought her to his chest. Samara held him tightly and sobbed. AJ finally figured it out. She wasn't terrified of *him*, at least not directly. She was terrified of being out of control, of being at the mercy of something bigger than she was. AJ was willing to bet Samara had never stepped one toe out of line, had never not crossed a "t" or not dotted an "i," She was the daughter, sister, friend, everyone relied on because she was dependable, and she needed to be that almost as much as they did. She was so reliable, she put her own plans on hold in order to be there for other people. Yet ever since she'd met him, Samara had started giving into her own whims, but she didn't have the guts to give into her biggest whim of all.

"Marry me," AJ whispered.

She sagged against him, and AJ held her tighter, bending his mouth to her ear. "Be my wife, Samara. Let me be your husband. You know you want me to be."

"Stop it," she whispered, and slapped his chest when he wouldn't let her wiggle out his embrace. "Stop it!"

"S'*agapo*, Samara. I love you. Marry me. Say you'll marry me and we can start a family of our own," AJ said.

"Please!" she croaked, shaking her head and wiggling even more. AJ allowed her the freedom she sought. She all but ran from him, and AJ didn't bother to catch up with her, though he made sure she was within his sights. She headed back to the hotel, and she took the elevator while he climbed the stairs.

Well, that hadn't gone as he had planned, but at least everything was now out in the open. Maybe he'd been too harsh, too aggressive. Samara already had a hard time standing up for herself, and he'd all but backed her into a corner and forced the most panicked declaration of love he'd ever heard from someone.

His laughter echoed in the stairwell, sounding as idiotic as he felt just then. Perhaps he was trying too hard, so insistent on the New Year's Eve fairytale that he forgot they were real people with real, complicated situations. How could he begrudge Samara's sense of responsibility to her family?

When AJ entered his room, he made a split-second decision. He went to his carry-on bag and pulled out the wine as well as the gift he'd gotten for Samara and Spyros's gift to Frankie. Checking his mobile briefly, he saw Dimitri had left a message. He listened to it quickly and frowned. *Oh, Dimitri...*he was so lucky he loved him, but AJ had to make one quick stop before he helped Dimitri out of trouble. There was something more pressing he had to do.

He went up the stairs to Samara's floor, and then went to her door and knocked.

Frankie looked at him with a bored expression. "Let me guess. Samara."

"Not right now," AJ said lowly, handing her Spyros's gift and the Greek wine. "For you. Well, not the wine. May I come in?"

Apparently, AJ's toneless directive exhibited his seriousness, so Frankie accepted the items and let him in without her customary battle. Samara had been sitting on the bed in a robe putting on lotion, and AJ, uncaring of Frankie's presence, dropped to his knees before her.

"AJ—?"

"This is a ticket to Greece, same flight as mine on the second. If you love me as you say you do...if you're willing to follow your heart and be happy, *agapi mou*, come with me. Rely on *me*, Samara. Depend on me and my love for you."

The indecision he saw in her eyes almost hurt more than a flat-out refusal, and Frankie's shocked gasp didn't give him much hope, either.

AJ didn't wait for either sister to say anything, merely kissed the backs of Samara's hands and left. He had to make sure at least one Melonakos's New Year started happily with the woman he loved.

TWELVE

As amused as he'd been, AJ had decided not to watch the destruction of Hurricane Landi once she realized Dimitri had broken into her home to make it the romantic enclave he hoped would soften her heart. He'd sustained some damage—Landi had an acerbic tongue at best and a downright evil streak at worst— but AJ was encouraged. At least Landi was talking to Dimitri now instead of granting him the silent treatment.

A silent Landi was not a pleasant Landi, merely the calm before the storm. Now that she'd released her fury, the cleanup could begin...that was, if she didn't make Dimitri a casualty.

AJ shook his head once he entered the elevator at the hotel. He had every faith in Dimitri as a Melonakos and in love in general. Things would end well for them. They had to, or else what was the point?

AJ refused to think of his own setbacks with Samara, or rather, the large roadblocks that were her family...herself. He didn't know what else he could do short of kidnapping her and whisking her away to Greece to show her how serious he was; and since Frankie *had* warned him their family was full of lawyers, he nixed that idea just as soon as it arrived. It would do him no good to be married to Samara and not be with her—conjugal visits be damned.

Nevertheless, AJ chuckled at the thought, slightly amused at the notion of serving time for taking what was rightfully his. His chuckles died down, however, when he approached his room and saw Samara in her pajamas sitting on the floor reading a book.

His Paul Laurence Dunbar collection.

"Samara?" he asked cautiously. What did this mean? She wasn't dressed to go out; but given the time, it was after eleven-thirty at the very least.

Samara made to stand and he helped her, grasping her hand gently in his. He didn't let go once she was settled on her feet.

"I told Frankie I wasn't feeling well," Samara said quietly and without preamble. "It wasn't a lie, but it wasn't a complete truth, either. I needed time to think."

AJ felt as if his lungs were in a vice, and he squeezed air out and sucked it into his body. "Okay…"

A deep breath. "Instead of me coming with you, why don't you come with me…to meet my family?" Samara asked in a rush.

Involuntarily, his hand squeezed hers in surprise. "What?"

"I asked if you wanted to meet my family…my parents."

"What are you really asking me, Samara?"

Samara blew out a breath and glared at him. "Look, I don't know if you know this or not, but women don't like ultimatums, especially *black* women. Shoot, we can do bad all by ourselves; and most of the time, it's not even a choice! But you listen and listen good, Alejandro Kyriakos Melonakos. Just because I love you, don't think your shit don't stink, got it?"

All he could do was blink at her. Had Samara met Landi and he not know about it? She was angry and upset, and AJ, for the life of him, couldn't figure out why. Ultimatums? He never gave her one!

"You don't want to be with me?" he asked, dazedly and dumbly.

"I want to do this right and without regrets," Samara said, her tone softening as she gazed upon him, "but you *will not* bully me to go halfway across the world without you showing your face to *my* family before I do it! I've never been with a man, so you need to realize that when you marry me, you're going to be married into my family. This is an audition for you too. To make sure you *really* want me."

"Of course I *really* want you," AJ said, glaring at her himself. "I love you! I want to marry you! I want to give you sons and daughters! I just don't understand why you keep giving me hoops to jump through as if I were a circus animal!"

Samara's eyes filled with hurt and AJ cursed himself. She nodded harshly and started toward the elevators. *No*, AJ thought. He knew Melonakos men could be singularly tracked, to the detriment of their own goals, but he wasn't going to lose Samara before he ever really had her. Forget his ego and pride.

"I'm sorry," AJ whispered atop her head as he brought her back to him. He wrapped his arms around her, his front to her back, and squeezed. "Damn it, Samara, you make me crazed!"

She didn't respond, but the shaky breath she emitted let him know she was dangerously close to tears. He buried his face in her neck and kissed her skin, feeling her tremble at the contact.

"I'm not going to let you walk away from me."

"And I'm not going to let you dictate the parameters of our relationship! I may be a novice at this, but I'm not a child, either!"

"If you were, I'd be in some deep shit."

To his surprise and pleasure, Samara turned her face into his arm and let out a giggle. "Lord, have mercy, AJ!"

Smiling, he kissed her jaw, and then pulled back and turned her around so they faced each other. "Can we continue this conversation in my room? I doubt the neighbors, all three of them who aren't out and about on such a night, want to hear our business."

"Business?" Samara's eyes widened, and her cheeks flushed. "Oh, dear."

Chuckling slightly, AJ bussed her forehead before unlocking his door and ushering them inside. Samara sat on the edge of the bed and, as before, AJ kneeled in front of her, his arms on either side of his thighs. This way, they were eye-level; but more importantly, AJ was humbling himself before her. Samara slid her hands along his cheeks and he closed his eyes, deathly afraid he wouldn't be able to feel her touch for another few weeks...months...perhaps more, after this trip.

"I thought Greeks were big on family," Samara mused aloud. AJ nodded and twisted his head to kiss the heel of her palm.

"We are."

"But you don't want to meet mine?"

"I'm afraid they'll keep you here with them instead of going to Greece with me."

"Why Greece?"

"I have family, a job in Greece."

"And I have family, a job in Philadelphia."

AJ shrugged. "You seemed happier when it was just you and me on the *Isis*. I just want you where you'll be the happiest."

Samara pursed her lips, her fingers moving idly over his cheek. She didn't seem like she was seeing him, but something else, some part of her past or possible future. He hoped she saw them together in that future.

"Frankie had earned a traveling grant from school for her major, and she wanted to go to Greece. Of course, our parents weren't too thrilled about their daughter going to a foreign, non-English-speaking country alone, so they gave me time off work to go with her. Frankie could use her grant, and I could do something for myself while keeping my parents from worrying to death."

AJ sighed, touching her jaw. "You were still on the job. You couldn't really enjoy yourself. You still had responsibilities."

"And if I'm with you, go with you, I will suddenly not have any? You know those children you seem so adamant on having? They won't be able to look after themselves when they're born; and once a parent, always a parent, even when your children are old enough to have children of their own."

She was right, and AJ knew it, but he was scared. "I don't want them to take you away from me."

"And I don't want to make you so impatient you'll find someone better," Samara admitted with a small smile.

"Impossible."

Her smile widened slightly and she shrugged. "Besides, you might change your mind anyway after you meet my family."

AJ cupped her cheek and matched her smile, his eyes soft and adoring. "Impossible."

Sighing, Samara's countenance grew gentle and she hugged AJ close. He returned the embrace just as fiercely, and the sounds of screaming and countdowns permeated their room despite the doors and windows being shut. Neither spoke as they pulled apart, their foreheads touching as they listened to the crowd shout, "HAPPY NEW YEAR!" amid cheers and honking horns. Silently, AJ captured her mouth with his and gave her a light, chaste kiss. Samara sighed again, her sweet, warm breath like a summer breeze to his soul. He increased the pressure of the kiss as he pressed forward, causing her to lie back on the bed. He rested his forearms on either side of her head and sank his fingers into her hair, and his hips undulated against hers. She moaned slightly, her legs opening to accommodate him.

She turned her face away with a sharp intake of breath, but AJ was undeterred, moving his mouth to her cheek and down the column of her throat. His hand slid down her torso, over the generous curve of her breast, to her round stomach and ending at her hip.

"I want to make love to you, Samara," he whispered against her jaw. "*Agapi mou…*"

Samara hugged him and AJ let out a shuddering breath against her collarbone. Her embrace was one of comfort and apology, and he accepted it. He knew there wouldn't be a consummation of their love now. But despite his body's yearnings, he knew it would mean so much more once they were officially husband and wife. And in order to get there, he would have to meet her family first.

In the meantime, however, AJ pulled down the covers, asking her to stay with his eyes. She gave him a gentle smile and nodded. As soon as she was settled underneath the covers, AJ bent and kissed her forehead.

"Happy New Year, *agapi mou*," he whispered against her temple.

"Happy New Year," she replied, and it didn't take her very long to fall asleep. AJ unclipped his mobile phone from his hip and called Frankie, telling her Samara would be spending the rest of the night with him.

"Is that right?" Frankie said amid the hoopla in the background.

"The first of many," AJ replied shortly, then smiled as he envisioned those future times. "Happy New Year, Frankie."

Frankie sucked her teeth but returned the sentiment. After putting his mobile in the charger, AJ took off his clothes, leaving himself in his boxers, and climbed into bed next to Samara. He grinned as she immediately found his body and snuggled into it, and that grin remained even as he fell asleep.

The next morning, Frankie, Samara, and AJ went to Penn Station. The sisters waited in the terminal, Samara calling home to say they were bringing a guest, while AJ purchased a last-minute ticket. Since the train was packed, AJ was sitting in an entirely different car from Samara. Before they boarded the train, AJ gave her a light kiss and told her he would see her in two hours.

He passed the time on the train talking to Spyros and his mother to wish them a Happy New Year, then reading more of *The Sea-Wolf*. His hands itched to dial Samara's number, but he refused. He could last two hours. Compared to the past few months, the hours should've felt like seconds.

Yes...thousands of seconds!

However, his misery soon ended and the train pulled into 30th Street Station in Philadelphia ninety minutes after leaving New York. Samara and Frankie were already in the terminal waiting for him, and he smiled.

"I can rent a car," AJ said, knowing Samara was too young to do so herself. They could've taken a taxi; but if things didn't go well with her family...

Samara blushed and hid her face. "Times like these I feel like a child!"

Chuckling, AJ kissed her forehead gently. "No, you're a woman, Samara. Don't ever forget that."

Frankie was suspiciously quiet, but she led the way to the car rental counters. AJ chose a midsize sedan for Samara's and Frankie's luggage. Though Frankie would go back the next day, she had laundry she wanted to do in the meantime. AJ had no luggage, and he'd called Dimitri to tell him where he would be during the day. He took the fact Dimitri's voicemail had picked up as a good sign.

The trio said little outside of Samara giving directions. They drove through downtown Philadelphia, Samara wanting to give him a tour of the city, and then they made their way to the northwest section of the city to the West Oak Lane neighborhood. They drove for a little bit until they reached a redbrick row house with a neatly clipped yard and a small set of stone stairs leading from the street to the front door.

"Do you live with your parents?" AJ asked, turning off the engine.

"I live downtown," Samara said, "but this is our New Year's dinner, and we have it at home."

AJ took the sisters' luggage from the trunk. "How will you get there?"

"There are taxis," Frankie said with a little snicker. "Don't worry, AJ. Samara's been doing this long before you came along."

Samara slammed the door of the rental car harder than she should have. "Girl, what's up with you!"

Frankie rolled her eyes and went ahead of them, muttering incoherently under her breath.

AJ could already tell this would turn out smashingly.

Happy greetings welcomed him and Samara as they entered the house and Frankie hugged her relatives. The chatter died down slightly, however, when the attention turned to them.

"Mommy," Samara breathed, right before wrapping her arms around a slender pecan-colored woman with a hairstyle like Frankie's. Samara's mother closed her eyes and took in the embrace fully, her maternal hands rubbing up and down her daughter's back.

"Happy New Year, my love," Samara's mother whispered.

"You, too, Mommy," Samara replied. She then hugged her aunt and her grandfather before coming back to AJ's side.

"Everyone, this is AJ," Samara said, and AJ intertwined their fingers together. She looked at him, suddenly at a loss of words, and AJ took mercy on her.

"Mrs. Grossman—"

"Fields," Samara's mother corrected. "And call me Sheryl."

"And call me, 'Auntie,' you *fine* tall drink o' water, you!" another woman said, taller and slimmer than Sheryl. Her skin was lighter and her hair was longer, too, straight and pulled back in a ponytail clasped at her nape. "Or Joyce. Whichever you prefer."

"Joyce!"

Joyce bumped Sheryl's hip. "I'm trying to make nice with my niece's friend, big sis. Isn't that what you said to do?"

The older man who was standing behind them all with Frankie stamped his cane on the ground and frowned. "Joyce. Behave."

Joyce merely winked in AJ's direction and gave a thumb up to Samara, who blushed furiously. The older man approached, and despite his cane and slight hunch, was still impressive in height and stature. He held out a strong hand for AJ to shake. "Gerald Fields, these young ladies' grandfather."

AJ stood straighter and accepted the offered hand. "I am Alejandro Melonakos and it is an honor to meet you."

"Hmm. And who else are you?"

"The man who loves your granddaughter with all his heart."

There was a collective gasp and one low whistle that followed that declaration, and Gerald's eyes narrowed. "Heard that line before, and my baby's heart got broken." There was a quick glance at Sheryl. "I'm even less inclined to believe it with you."

"Why?"

"Outside the fact you're older and white? You want to take my baby out the country. I don't like that idea at all."

"Frankie!" Samara said, shooting her secret-divulging sister an unpleasant look.

"Don't yell at her," Gerald said, frowning at his oldest grandchild. "At least you had the decency to introduce your young man to us *before* you married him."

Sheryl's eyes went downcast and Joyce bit her lip. "I think we'll check on the ham," Joyce said, hooking her arm through Sheryl's and leading them away, pausing only to grab Frankie on the way there. Gerald pointed his cane into the living room to their left.

"Come sit. We have much to discuss before we eat. Sheryl! Get this young man some water."

AJ knew better than to ignore the order. He made sure Samara remained next to him so she'd know she wouldn't face her family alone.

"So. You think you love my granddaughter after only five days of knowing her," Gerald said, cutting directly to the chase as soon as he sat in a worn, dark-brown easy chair.

"I knew after the first day, but didn't fully admit it to myself until after the fourth," AJ confessed.

Samara's gasp and sudden tension pulled AJ's gaze from her grandfather to her, and her awed expression brought a smile to his face. AJ kissed Samara's knuckles. "That's true."

"Why her?" Gerald said, pointing the bottom of his cane towards Samara. "You're a handsome young man in Europe. Surely there are numerous beautiful women you could prey upon—"

"I'm not sure which insinuation is more insulting—the fact you don't think your granddaughter is beautiful, or the fact you don't think I can show women respect," AJ said, his tone growing menacing and dark. Samara's grandfather or no, he would give Samara the proper reverence.

"I know she's beautiful," Gerald said with a scowl, as if AJ's comment had offended him.

"When's the last time you told her such? How often do you do so?" AJ asked, nodding his thanks to Samara's mother when she brought the glass of water.

"Looks aren't everything," Gerald said. "What good is a pretty face if she has nothing behind it?"

"Your granddaughters aren't dunces, either. They are very beautiful and intelligent women. I can't understand why they're so afraid of their power—*especially* Samara!" AJ said, his voice rising with his frustration.

"That power can be exploited," Gerald said, his own tone growing cold. His eyes skipped to Sheryl, and she shook her head. "It's better for a woman not to let on how strong she is lest she be taken advantage of.

Especially black women. *Especially* black women with suave white men!"

AJ frowned as he looked at Samara. "Is your father white?"

"No, but he likes white women—*ouch!* Stop slapping me!" Joyce said, frowning at her sister and rubbing her right oblique gingerly.

"It's better that she focuses on her career and herself before she focuses on men," Sheryl said quietly. "Get herself together and in a position to be comfortable just in case a romance goes awry. I don't want her to be picking up the pieces like I did. And thank goodness she doesn't have any kids—"

"And the way to do that is to pile responsibility and guilt upon responsibility and guilt on her until she has no time to think of love and *her* happiness? Keep her working for you so she doesn't know there's a whole world out there waiting for her?" AJ queried, trying very hard not to glower at them.

Joyce's eyes snapped fire. "I don't think I like your tone!"

"And I *know* I don't like the way you've made Samara feel she's not good enough!" AJ shot back, completely forgetting this was his love's family. "She has no sense of herself as a woman, and if I were any more of a cad, I *would've* exploited her vulnerability! Not every man she meets will be her father!"

"Clearly," Gerald scoffed, rolling his eyes.

"Well, at least she's not gay like you thought, Dad," Joyce said, trying to expose a bright side. "You were really concerned when she went natural and cut off all her hair—"

"Unbelievable!" Samara muttered, pinching the bridge of her nose.

"Especially that you're letting him sit there and talk to us like that!" Joyce finished.

"I'm only saying what she's too scared to say for fear you'll reject her!" AJ said, glaring at all of them, including Frankie. "Instead of being supportive and encouraging, you've been the exact opposite! She's a grown woman, now—a grown woman in love with a white, older man from Greece! And she's *happy*! So, are you going to let your daughter, granddaughter, sister, and niece finally live her life as she sees fit wholeheartedly, or will you condemn her for that as well?"

Samara was shaking, trembling so violently that AJ stood and forced her to do the same. He walked out of the charged den into the foyer, needing to get Samara out of that environment. No wonder Samara was afraid of love and happiness—she'd been taught to fear it! It seemed Samara had gotten the brunt of the lessons because Frankie and Joyce, being the younger sisters, and probably by some standards the more beautiful of the two, appeared to have more freedom and more sense of self. Sheryl and Samara, on the other hand, did as they were told, even if it went against their own wishes. AJ wondered if Sheryl's choice in Samara and Frankie's father was because of true feelings or an act of rebellion.

Probably a little of both...*just like Samara.*

AJ framed Samara's face, his heart breaking at the tears standing in her eyes.

"Come away with me," he whispered. "Right now. Show your grandfather, your family, you aren't afraid to follow your heart."

Panic filled her eyes and Samara's body shook. AJ chastised himself. Wasn't he doing what her grandfather was doing? Giving her orders, telling her what to do? All for "her best interests?" AJ could concede Samara's family loved her, for it just wanted to equip her with all the tools to help her make it through life's troubled times. But what about those good times? Did she have the tools to live through those too?

"I think I should go," AJ said quietly, his thumb stroking her cheeks. When Samara began to protest, AJ kissed her lips to silence her. "You need time to work things out for yourself and with your family. And me, in my impatience to start our life together, didn't understand that. But I do now." He kissed her again, longer this time. "I don't want you coming to me with regrets, just as you said yesterday, so...no ultimatums, no pressure, just the hope that sooner...*much* sooner rather than later, you'll be in my arms wearing my last name and carrying my seed within your womb."

"Damn! Maybe I need to go to Greece!"

Samara and AJ snapped toward the voice to see Samara's family watching them avidly. AJ thought he could see the glimmer of approval in Sheryl's eyes, but Gerald still regarded him as if he were Lucifer's reincarnate.

AJ approached all the women and kissed their knuckles, spending extra time on Sheryl's hand, and then stopped in front of Gerald.

"I love Samara, sir," AJ began, his eyes firm as they stared into the dark-brown of Gerald's. "But you all need to talk without me here. So I will leave, and I thank you for having me as a guest. I just want you to know I do plan on Samara being my wife, with or without your permission, but I know it would mean so much to her if she had it."

He bowed slightly before Gerald in a show of deference. Once he stood tall again, he went to Frankie. It was only now he realized she wore the earrings Spyros had sent her. Opals, for her birth month.

"Good luck," Frankie said, as if it pained her to do so.

AJ gave her an understanding smile. "You'll be all right, Frankie."

Frankie looked like she was barely hanging on, and AJ pulled her into his arms for a large hug. "Be on Samara's side for once," AJ said for her ears only, ignoring her indignant gasp. "Free trips to Greece...and Spyros..."

Frankie sniffled. "So confident."

"Call me an optimist," AJ said, and kissed the top of her head. "Do well in school."

"Okay, Dad," Frankie said, rolling her eyes.

"Big brother," AJ said, brushing the tears away from her cheek. "I've always wanted a little sister."

A genuine smile graced Frankie's face as she nodded. "I think you'd make an excellent big brother."

"And I'll make an excellent husband too," AJ said, looking pointedly first as Gerald, then back to Samara, who had her eyes downcast. He went to her. "I'm not your father, baby. I'm your man. Don't you ever forget it, either."

Then, AJ gave her a kiss that made sure she wouldn't, a kiss that could've escalated to something indecent had Gerald not shoved his cane into the floor with enough force to almost put a hole through it. As soon as AJ pulled away, Samara tore upstairs, Sheryl following immediately. No one followed AJ to the car, which was just as well. He didn't know if he could remain polite to the rest of Samara's family. Just as he was pulling away from the curb, his mobile phone rang.

Dimitri.

AJ's voice was monotonous as he answered. "I'm returning to Greece, cousin. Alone."

THIRTEEN

The drive back to the train station had been hard, as well as the even lonelier train ride back to Penn Station. Dimitri had met AJ there, and he gave him an encouraging pat on the back.

"It'll work out," Dimitri said. "New Year, new beginnings."

AJ said that phrase like a mantra as he boarded his plane back to Athens the next day; during the subsequent days where he received not so much as an e-mail from Samara; during the weeks when the restaurant had gotten so busy that all he could do was wake up and go to bed from exhaustion. Returning to Greece had been torture, much as it had been when Samara had left the first time. Yet this time, there weren't any long conversations on the phone, IM, or webcam. It was as if Samara had been completely cut off from him, and all calls or e-mails to her remained unanswered.

AJ threw himself into his work, so much so he didn't even realize it was February until Spyros entered his bedroom blowing a kazoo and throwing confetti in his bed.

"Get up, you old coot! Happy Birthday! Thirty-five today!"

AJ shuddered and threw an aimless pillow in Spyros's direction. "Go to hell."

"After you," Spyros said cheekily. "And you're one year closer to it yourself! Thirty-five! You're as old as the Acropolis!" Spyros cackled, and blew the kazoo in the most irritating manner known to humankind.

"Happy Birthday, indeed," AJ murmured, his eyes going to the painting that now hung on the wall across from him so it would be the first thing he saw every morning. His heart constricted painfully as his eyes took in him and Samara together, then looked at the cold, empty space next to him.

"Happy Birthday, indeed."

AJ showered and dressed as normal, thinking it was very fitting his birthday fell on a Monday this year. At least he could hide his despondency in his work, but he knew better than to be completely surly. His mother lived for birthdays; and considering he was her only child, he would try to be excited about the day for her benefit. Besides, this was the anniversary of her motherhood as well as his birth. As such, a sincere smile did form on his face when he thought of the gift he'd bought for her. Every year, since his eighteenth birthday, AJ had given his mother a gift on his birthday to celebrate her day, thinking it belonged to her as much as it belonged to him. This year, he'd gotten them plane tickets to go to Santa Monica to visit Aunt Airlia and Uncle Feodras in May, right before the Athens tourist season started. It had been far too long since they'd seen them, which had been at Khristos's funeral almost two years ago.

AJ bounded down the stairs and walked to the restaurant. As soon as he entered, he was bombarded with well wishes and benign ribbing. His uncle, Spyros's father, gave him a cane with a shiny blue bow on it, and AJ let out a genuine laugh. His Uncle Andros had always had a fantastic sense of humor.

"We're closing early, party tonight to celebrate my favorite nephew!" Uncle Andros said laughingly as he gave AJ a hug.

"Hey!" Anatole exclaimed indignantly.

Uncle Andros laughed again. "AJ doesn't hear it when I say it to *you*, does he?"

After that, AJ's day turned out to be surprisingly wonderful, definitely the best day of the New Year by far. His mother stole a moment of privacy with him and they hugged in his office for a very long time.

"I'm proud of you, *mijo*," Luz said in a mixture of Greek and Spanish.

AJ kissed the top of his mother's head and squeezed her tighter. "You're my first love, Mama. Never forget that."

Luz grasped her son's chin with a quick, gentle pressure before patting him maternally on his backside. "Break's over. Get back to work."

Perhaps it was because the restaurant closed earlier that day, but AJ didn't feel nearly as exhausted as he had been for the past few weeks at the end of the workday. In fact, his mood was light as Spyros pulled him down into the seat of honor and the employees brought a cake out with thirty-five sparkling candles. Luz ran her fingers through his hair, looking upon her son with pure adoration and pride. Family. He'd been living in his funk and missing Samara so much that he'd forgotten he had an entire host of people who loved him.

"Thank you," AJ whispered, his throat uncharacteristically tight before he blew out the candles with two breaths.

For the next hour, everyone ate and talked and danced. Luz absolutely loved her present and told him she was going off to call Aunt Airlia with the news. Ana pulled AJ from the table and encouraged him to dance, and he surrendered to the merriment of the day. He was enjoying himself so much that he almost missed the piercing whistle that brought everything to a halt. Knowing it had come from Spyros, he glared at his cousin, who shrugged and pointed frantically to his mother.

"I haven't given you my gift yet, *mijo*," Luz said with a soft, loving smile on her face.

AJ looked at the table, then back to his mother with a frown. "Mama?"

"Happy Birthday—oh!" Luz laughed, surprised when AJ lifted her off her feet and hugged her tightly. The rest of the party laughed as well, but AJ's ears had homed onto one laugh in particular, the one belonging to the one person he never thought he would see.

"*Agapitos*," AJ breathed, his hands shaking fiercely as they cupped the brown cheeks he hadn't touched in four weeks.

"*Novio*," Samara said in return, two hot tears falling down her face. "That is, if you still want me..."

AJ's kiss was all the answer she needed.

AJ didn't ask how or why she was here with him on his birthday, and he really didn't care, but his mother had told him she'd been in contact with Sheryl since the week after he'd come home all sad faced and depressed. Sheryl had looked up their information from their website and had called the restaurant on a whim, asking to speak with AJ or his mother. Luz had answered the phone, and the two ladies had spent a long time discussing their children and how they would get them back together.

"She saw how unhappy her daughter was, *mijo*," Luz said, smiling at AJ who held Samara on his lap, refusing to let her go. They were in the office while his birthday celebration still carried on in the dining area, this time AJ and Samara in the office chair at Luz's insistence. "And it seemed your speech impressed her," Luz added.

"Mama said she wished my father would've fought for her like that," Samara murmured, pressing her cheek against his.

"I'll always fight for you," AJ vowed, kissing her lips lightly. "And I'll always love you."

"I love you too."

Samara would return to Philadelphia on Friday as she was only here for AJ's birthday, but he demanded she stay with him until then. Samara, of course, blushed at this edict while Luz rolled her eyes, but his mother was adamant she and Samara have a few moments to get to know each other.

His entire family and employees practically formed a line to meet Samara when they returned to the party. AJ had been concerned she would get a lukewarm response because she wasn't Greek, but he should've known his mother would've prepared them of that fact. Then again, he was the only one who'd seemed surprised by Samara's arrival. He supposed when the Melonakos clan had to keep a secret, they could!

"We got you good, didn't we, cousin?" Spyros asked, slapping his back.

"Yeah, now that I think about it," AJ said, eyes narrowed as Luz and Samara spoke with Ana and Spyros's mother. "You aren't normally so cheery on my birthday."

Spyros beamed. "It's good to see you happy again. You were depressing as hell these last few weeks!"

AJ shrugged and wrapped one arm around Spyros's shoulder, then his other arm around Anatole who'd come to join them. "I don't think I will be any longer, gentlemen."

That night, AJ made love to Samara with his mouth and hands and she did the same. After they experienced ecstasy, AJ held her nude body against his and asked her to marry him again.

"Yes," she replied, caressing her hand over his heart. "I would love to be your wife."

AJ took a series of deep breaths before placing a tender kiss to her temple. "I don't have a ring."

"I don't need a ring," she insisted, cupping his jaw to bring his mouth to hers. "Just you."

They planned to have the wedding a year to the day of when they'd first met, right in the restaurant. He did catch a bit of flak for not having a Greek Orthodox wedding, but he respectfully told his elders to back off. Both he and Samara tried to cover all the costs themselves, but their mothers refused to be left out of the planning. Luckily, they both had great ideas, so Samara and AJ were happy with the results.

A few days before the wedding, he and Samara went shopping for rings. AJ had thought about getting the engagement ring himself, but he wanted Samara to have input on their bands. Luz had offered to give him her engagement ring from his father, but AJ had kissed his mother's forehead and told her to keep it.

"Oh, AJ..." Samara breathed when they found her engagement ring. It was a two-carat Asscher-cut diamond with diamonds studded in the band. He'd spotted it on the opposite end of the counter they were browsing and knew it would be the one. They also got matching white-gold wedding bands to complete the set.

"All of a sudden, it's become more real," she whispered as he slipped her engagement ring on her finger.

Her words resonated with AJ right up to the big day. The weight of what was about to happen, of the amount of responsibility and duty that loomed before him, made AJ's mood uncharacteristically somber. This was the single-most important event of his life, and he prayed to God he wouldn't mess it up.

In the next thirty minutes, he would be someone's husband. More importantly, he would be *her* husband, the shy American woman he'd spotted in the market a year to the day before. A simple grocery run, it should have been, but he'd found Samara instead. Extremely blessed for the discovery, he'd followed her, come on a little strong, he knew, but time had been of the essence. There'd been no way he would let Samara leave without her knowing just who he was...who *she* was.

Loved.

At first sight, she'd taken his heart and he hadn't wanted it back, just hers in return. The moment they'd locked eyes, he'd known he'd have it, even if it would take a while for her to surrender it. This hadn't been because she hadn't trusted *him*, but rather because she hadn't trusted the circumstances that had brought them together in the first place.

A chance meeting in a country where she barely knew the language...a country she'd only intended to visit, not to live...a family who wouldn't understand any of it, especially when she couldn't herself. And yet, she was currently upstairs in Spyros's parents' flat donning a dress for a ceremony that would make her his wife.

For the first time all day, AJ smiled.

"About time! For a second we thought we were attending a funeral!"

He cut his eyes to his cousins, scowling briefly before the grin reappeared.

Rest in peace, single Alejandro Kyriakos Melonakos. You won't be missed!

AJ was just as bewitched seeing Samara walking toward him to be married as she'd been when he saw her in Monastiraki. Bringing up the rear behind a very pretty Frankie, she had a bouquet of cliff roses and an orchid in her hair, and her wedding dress was the same style and cut as the summer dress she'd worn on that first day he'd seen her, except it was white this time. On her feet were white mules and her toenails were painted clear. Spyros and Dimitri had to remind him to breathe, but she'd taken all of his breath away when she smiled brightly at him.

The ceremony was brief, but the kiss at the end of it was certainly the opposite. AJ couldn't stop kissing his *wife*, and Samara had been disinclined to make him. Dimitri had to yank him away from Samara to stop it, and only Samara's laughter joining in with everyone else's prevented a murder from occurring on the happiest day of AJ's life.

The reception was lively, but AJ and Samara slipped out while it was still going strong. His mother had ordered a car to take them to the marina where they would spend their very first night as husband and wife on the *Isis*.

"My goodness, AJ, it's beautiful!" Samara murmured when they stepped aboard the vessel. There were flameless candles strategically placed all aboard the deck with a bottle of Lysimelis and a basket of food on a white blanket adorned with white rose petals waiting for them.

He smiled softly and kissed her lips. "You're infinitely more beautiful, Samara."

By the time AJ had sailed the *Isis* into "their lagoon" and dropped anchor, the sun had already set. The flameless candles provided more than enough light as the wedded couple ate from the basket Melonakos had prepared. The air had gotten considerably colder, which provided AJ ample excuse to hold his wife close as he fed her black seedless grapes one by one. Eventually, they abandoned the food altogether and started kissing each other earnestly. Then suddenly, Samara broke away and stood before him, the shadows and illumination on her body making AJ's mouth go dry from her loveliness.

Hands trembling slightly, Samara kept her eyes on his as she started to disrobe. AJ didn't move anything but his eyes as article after article of clothing hit the deck. Then, she was gloriously nude before him, her hands balling up into fists even as a small smile filled her face.

Staring at her in awe, AJ walked on his knees before her and kissed her belly.

"I want to give you a baby tonight," he confessed against her skin.

She laughed. "Seriously?"

He pulled back and grinned. "Why wait?"

She shook her head and sighed with exasperation, but AJ made her catch her breath when his hands slid to her bum and cupped it. One hand then drifted between her thighs and found her already soaking wet. He hummed against her navel as he lifted one leg over his shoulder before bending his head to press a sweet kiss to her center.

"AJ," she whispered, her fingers gripping his hair.

He curled his tongue out and gave her one long lap, collecting her feminine dew. She was hot, soft, damp, and tasty. Samara trembled and pressed his face closer. AJ inhaled her scent and groaned, then circled his tongue around the hard nubbin above her entrance. He loved her fully and completely with his tongue and mouth, adding his fingers to thrust into her to make her reach her climax. It had only taken a minute for her to come, and AJ helped ease her onto the deck when her legs could no longer support her.

As soon as her neck came level, he pressed his mouth against her pulse point and pulled her close.

"You taste delicious, *agapitos*," he murmured, then pressed his lips against hers. Samara started tugging his shirt from his pants and her hands blazed a path along his abdomen.

"Off," she muttered, her fingers undoing the fly and zip of his slacks.

"Eager, are we?" AJ asked with a chuckle while his mouth drifted down her body to capture a nipple.

"Yes. I want you inside me, AJ," she said in a trembling voice, clasping his head to her chest.

AJ pulled back long enough to disrobe, but he wasn't quick enough to stop Samara from wrapping a hand around his hardened length and stroking it. He allowed her to do this for a few moments; but when her mouth closed around him, he jerked back abruptly.

"AJ?" she asked, hurt strong in her voice.

He fell to his knees before her and cupped her face in his hands. "It'll be all over before we start if you suck me, *agapi mou*."

She ducked her head but flashed him a grin, caressing his hardness again. "Can't have that..."

AJ arched an eyebrow and slid his fingers inside her essence. "No, we can't."

He gently settled her onto her back and rose above her. The head of his erection grazed her core, and both shuddered with anticipation. He stared at her for a moment, watching the light flicker over her form, and he didn't think she'd ever been more beautiful. He cupped her face and kissed her gently, lining himself up at her opening.

"Are you ready, Samara?"

She nodded.

AJ entered her with one, strong thrust. Samara froze and tensed underneath him, her sharp gasp almost shattering his heart. He framed her face and brushed away the tears that streamed from her closed eyes while he remained still inside her. He whispered reassurances in Greek while dotting her face with kisses. She was so tight and wet around him, and his body shook with the need to move. He remained still, however, until she got used to his invasion. The last thing he wanted was to injure her because of his passions.

She blew out a breath and laughed harshly. "And women *like this*?"

He frowned, smoothing a hand over her head. "It'll get better, Samara. Do you want me to pull out?"

She didn't answer immediately, but then she shook her head and cupped his jaw. "No, I'll be fine. It's starting to feel a little better."

"*Eisaste ouranos*," he whispered into her palm. "You are heaven."

Samara moaned and squeezed her internal muscles around him, causing him to groan. AJ began to gently pump his hips, moving his mouth up to wrap his lips around her ring-adorned finger on her left hand. Samara spread her thighs wider to accommodate him, and soon they were gasping and panting from lovemaking. He shifted onto his back and Samara straddled him, looking at him with lust and uncertainty, but he gripped her hips and guided her movements along his erection. She caught his rhythm quickly, and soon he was sitting up to kiss her mouth, her neck, her breasts, as he felt his release hurtle toward him.

"AJ!" she gasped, her fingernails digging into his neck.

He nipped her throat. "Come on, baby, come for me, *agapi mou...*"

She did, most vibrantly, her sweat-slicked body bowing from the force of her orgasm. AJ was directly behind her, shooting his seed deep within her body. He collapsed onto the soft blanket beneath them, keeping her close to his chest. They breathed heavily as his hand caressed her bare back in sweeping circles.

"I get it now," Samara murmured after a brief stretch of silence.

"Get what, precious?" AJ asked, trailing his finger along the bridge of her nose.

"Why women like it. It feels *good*, AJ, *really good!*"

He chuckled and kissed her nose. "You might not be saying that in the morning; I suspect you'll be rather sore."

"My man's a big man," Samara sang, laughing against his mouth.

"My woman's a tight, sexy woman," he returned, kissing her intensely and feeling his length harden again.

They made love once more on the deck before moving below to the main sleeping cabin and making love again. And as he drew her exhausted and sleepy form close after experiencing yet another earth-shattering release, AJ prayed fervently this day and night hadn't just been another one of his dreams.

AJ woke up slowly to a gentle rocking. It took him a few moments to realize he was on the *Isis*, and the sun was just starting its languid rise into the sky. Groaning, he stretched, the covers tangling in his legs. He could tell today would be another beauty.

He didn't want to get out of bed.

The off-season months were usually the best to go boating. While there would always be tourists, springtime was perfection. It was warm, but not too warm; the days were getting longer; and the spirit of renewal was universal. To AJ, nothing was more renewing that spending the day in bed; however, that wasn't to be. Even on his self-imposed vacation, he had duties and responsibilities, and Spyros knew AJ wouldn't be of much use to the restaurant until he could take the *Isis* out during the first of spring. It had been AJ's tradition from the moment he'd gotten the boat, and he wouldn't stop it now that he was the primary owner of the restaurant. AJ knew he'd done well by choosing his formerly irresponsible cousin to manage Melonakos.

Nude and mindful of his height, AJ got out of bed and left the cabin. Through the windows he'd left open, he smelled the sea breeze and smiled.

Well, perhaps it wasn't so bad that he had to wake, after all.

The smile still on his face, AJ went above deck. He closed his eyes and took a hearty breath, only to open them when he heard splashing and laughter.

He peered over the side of the boat into the water and his smile grew even more. A child, his face alight with the world's sweetest smile and body full of joyous shrieks and giggles, kicked tiny little legs toward his mother's waiting, encouraging arms. Both cheered at his accomplishment once he reached his mother's safe embrace, and then she rewarded her son with bountiful kisses and hearty snuggles.

"My little *psari!*" she cooed, laughing when her son rubbed his face in her neck. "I gave birth to a fish!"

"*Mana!*" the toddler cried, giggling as his mother rubbed her face into his neck in return.

"Decided to beat the sun to the water again, I see," AJ said, leaning on the railing of the yacht. Mother and child looked up at his comment, and the little boy squealed and clapped.

"*Baba!*" The little boy held out his honey-hued arms.

The mother chuckled and kissed her son's temple as she swam to the ladder of the boat. "That's a view."

"A beautiful view," AJ agreed, going to the ladder as well. "Why didn't you wake me? I would've loved to greet the sun with you." He climbed down to meet them; and as soon as they reached him, he bent down to accept the kiss his son bestowed on him and took him in his arms.

"Naked as the day you were born," AJ murmured, climbing back up to the deck. His son giggled more and snuggled into his father's strong bare chest. "Just like your *mana*."

"AJ."

"Samara," AJ returned, amused she could still blush despite the fact he was well, and happily, acquainted with her bare form. He watched her progress up the ladder, breathless as the water clung to her skin while sliding down her body...over the gentle swell ensconcing their second child. AJ got to his knees before her and kissed her tummy, causing her to laugh slightly and slide her fingers through his hair. Not to be left out, their son mimicked his father's actions, though he wasn't nearly so reverent.

"Your *adelfi* is in there, *gios*," AJ whispered to his son against Samara's navel.

"You don't know that," Samara said, her fingers dancing over AJ's ear. "Could be a boy again, his *adelfos*."

"You promised me a girl this time," AJ said and smiled against her skin at her scoff.

"Not up to me. I just push them out. A baby factory—"

"No," AJ said, traces of his teasing gone as he stood. Since she was still on the top rung of the ladder, they were more level than usual, but Samara still had to tilt her head back to look him in the eye. "You are my love, my wife, and the mother of my children. A manufacturer is the last thing I consider you to be."

Her eyes filled with love, and like their son, she nuzzled her face in his chest. "I love you, too, *esposo*."

Without letting her go, AJ made sure she got fully in the boat, then hugged her tighter when she was steady. AJ didn't think he could get any happier, but he knew he would in five months, when their next little bundle entered the world. His life, his family was in his arms. Who knew a routine trip to the market four years ago would lead to his destiny?

About the Author

Originally from Blythewood, South Carolina, Savannah J. Frierson has been writing since she was twelve years old, releasing her debut novel *Being Plumville* in March 2007 with iUniverse, Inc. She has released more publications since then, and they are available at online book retailers or by request at brick and mortar bookstores. For more information about other titles, please visit Savannah's website at http://www.sjfbooks.com or contact Savannah by e-mail at me@sjfbooks.com.

You can also join Savannah's newsletter at https://www.subscribepage.com/sjfbooks and support her Patreon page at http://www.patreon.com/sjfbooks to get sneak peeks, exclusive reads, and other goodies.

Excerpt from *Dimitri's Moon*

She'd been at the park for a few hours enjoying the attractions. Her cell rang as she dodged a small child and his rapidly melting ice cream cone. "Hello?"

"Afternoon, gorgeous."

Landi stepped to the side and smiled at Dimitri's voice. "Hey, yourself. How're you doing?"

"I'm better now. Where are you?"

"I'm by the Coconut Bay Café. How about you?"

"On my way to you."

Sensual shivers spread throughout her despite the warmth of the day. Dimitri had this way of sounding so damn sexy when he talked. "I'll be waiting," she said softly before disconnecting the call. Landi sat down on the edge of a bench and watched the steady flow of people before her.

As if the entire park shifted from normal to slow-motion, her gaze landed upon Dimitri Melonakos advancing toward her. Her breath caught in her throat, her heart skipped a few beats, and the juncture between her legs grew damp with longing. The man strode with an inherent confidence that drew many appreciative stares.

His black hair caught the breeze and bounced with each powerful step he took. A dark-blue shirt conformed to his impressive torso; his biceps strained against the sleeves. He had on light blue jeans that hugged powerful thighs. Though he exuded power, Dimitri had a lazy smile on his face when he stopped before her.

Landi stood to meet him and enjoyed the envious looks some women sent her as his arms closed around her. He smelled fresh and crisp.

"*Kalispera*, Landi," he whispered as he kissed her lightly.

The amount of passion that rocketed through her weakened her knees. Her arms wrapped around his waist as she kissed him back. A frustrated moan slipped from her lips when he put some space between them.

"How are you, baby?"

"I'm fine," she said, dropping her arms from around his trim waist. Her eyes dropped to his chest and she smiled. "Nice shirt."

"Thanks. One of my faves."

The shirt had a marbled look to it with the head of a Great White Shark across it. The animal looked like it was breaking through the fabric.

Very fitting," she commented as he took her hand. Landi recalled his Team had taken its nickname from that of a prehistoric shark, one thought to be the largest and deadliest carnivorous creature of the oceans. It tripled the size of today's Great White; in fact, experts thought it to be the Great White's ancestor.

He smiled down at her. "You look beautiful, Landi. And so hot!"

She ducked her head to hide her reddening cheeks. Only Dimitri could make her blush like a schoolgirl. "Thank you," she muttered, glad he thought so. In the back of her mind, she knew she'd wanted to impress him.

As if he sensed she was uncomfortable, he questioned, "Where'd you want to go?"

Tucking a wayward curl behind her ear, Landi tipped her head up. "Have you eaten?"

"Not since 0530."

Her brows furrowed. "When'd you leave this morning?"

His lips brushed hers. "Much sooner than I wanted to."

That damn blush and tingly feeling swept her body. "Do you want to eat here?" she asked, pointing toward the Coconut Bay Café.

"Here's just fine."

Hand in hand, they walked to the restaurant and had a nice lunch. Afterward, they went next door into the Shark Encounter. As the sharks swam over the top of them, Landi looked on in awe and wonder.

"They truly are so graceful," she said as Dimitri stepped away from her a bit to allow a little boy to run between them.

"They are. Almost enough so that you forget what amazing predators they are. There's an eerie ghost-like quality to them."

Leaning against the railing, Landi nodded. "Still, they are beautiful."

"No argument."

Dimitri wrapped his arm around her waist and they continued on. Her gaze traveled over multitudes of sand tiger, blacktip, whitetip, and bonnethead sharks. Even though they'd been safe, Landi still felt better once the warm California sun touched her skin. The sharks had this power about them that made her nervous.

The couple attended the Dolphin Interaction Program; and as her fingers moved across a dolphin's back, Landi felt totally at peace. Being with Dimitri gave her that. They watched the dolphin show while holding hands. As they left their seats, Dimitri gazed down at her and queried, "Where to now?"

"Polar bears."

"As milady commands.

For more on Dimitri and Landi's story, visit Aliyah Burke's website at http://aliyah-burke.com/books/mt/dimitrismoon.htm and sign up for her newsletter at http://aliyah-burke.com/newsletter.htm. Enjoy the Megalodon Team and all of Aliyah's other great reads!

www.ingramcontent.com/pod-product-compliance
Lightning Source LLC
Chambersburg PA
CBHW070628170726
48291CB00003B/923